As an only child growing up Ruth Baker Walton enjoyed a freedom that few young children today can experience. Not only did she acquire a love of nature, but it also fuelled a vivid imagination.

At school, Ruth's most successful subjects were English, Geography and Art, although she never acquired a love of school itself. This has not prevented her from achieving certain successes in her life. She has raised two daughters and, together with her husband, has run a successful business for over 40 years.

Ruth was Chairman and then President of The Wildlife Art Society Intl. until a few years ago. During her time with the society, she received a number of awards, the pinnacle of which was the 2008 Christopher Parsons Award for Artistic Excellence.

Ruth has been fortunate to visit Africa annually for over 20 years, which provided the inspiration for much of her art and also for her debut novel. From these experiences, she has written articles published by the society's magazine and the Kenya Airways Inflight magazine, Msafiri. Ruth regularly gives illustrated talks about her travels and art and recently self-published a book of poetry inspired by the natural world. Writing allows her to express her creativity through a different medium and to explore the depths of her imagination in a way art does not.

Dedicated to my long-suffering husband, and our two daughters, Gabriella and Julia.

Ruth Baker Walton

THE SECRET OF ROOKERY MANOR

AUSTIN MACAULEY PUBLISHERS™

LONDON • CAMBRIDGE • NEW YORK • SHARJAH

A CIP catalogue record for this title is available from the British Library.

ISBN 9781528970693 (Paperback)
ISBN 9781528974578 (ePub e-book)

www.austinmacauley.com

First Published 2024
Austin Macauley Publishers Ltd®
1 Canada Square
Canary Wharf
London
E14 5AA

Introduction

The young girl looked around the now empty room and sighed. In a few days she would be in a different world, starting a new life far away from here. She had one more task to do and ran along the corridor, opened the door at the far end and climbed the stairs. The attic room at the top was large, a single light bulb and a tiny window at the far end were the only source of light. Close to the window stood a large rocking horse and beside it lay a small trunk. The girl stroked the rocking horse fondly.

"I hope the new owners will look after you," she whispered into its ear. "I'm entrusting you to guard these precious possessions until the right one comes to collect them." Opening the trunk she carefully laid a small book, wrapped in a red silk scarf, on top of the other items already there.

"Rebecca, Rebecca, where are you? We are about to leave." A voice called out from somewhere below.

"Coming, Mother." The girl replied. Patting the rocking horse once more, she wiped a tear from her face and hurried down the stairs.

Chapter 1 –
Rookery Manor

Sitting in the back of his father's car as it sped through the narrow country lanes, James thought his life would never be the same again. Thanks to his parents, he was being up-rooted from friends he had known all his 12 years to leave London and live in a village called Stanton Seymour somewhere in Somerset. 'I bet they're all farmers and walk about all day in Welly Boots smelling of cow pats,' thought James glumly staring out of the window, 'Probably never even been to London!'

His mother on the other hand could hardly contain herself talking excitedly to his father about their plans. Adele Devonshire had always fancied herself as "A Lady of the Manor" and now thanks to her husband's decision to leave the city, she soon would be. The moment she laid eyes on Rookery Manor she had fallen in love with its well-proportioned stone walls, mullioned windows, tall brick-built chimneys and the long sweeping driveway. James suddenly became aware of his father's voice talking to him.

"You'll really love it James and you can always have your friends down to stay during school holidays."

"The gardens are enormous," his mother chipped in, "you'll have great fun playing games when they visit and I am sure you'll soon make new friends in the village."

James however was *not* so sure and continued to stare blankly out of the car window. He was an only child, the sort of person you wouldn't notice in a crowd, intelligent but quiet with his father's dark hair and brown eyes.

Three hours ago, he had watched his father close the door on their Kensington home for the last time. The removal van had left with their belongings and was now making its way towards Somerset.

"We're here!" his mother exclaimed excitedly. "Oh look James, isn't it lovely."

Begrudgingly he had to admit it did look lovely. The stone walls shone a warm mellow ochre in the glow of the late afternoon sun. The house looked enormous, much bigger than the house in Kensington. As the car swept up the driveway James could see the removal van was already there, unloading their furniture. He also noticed an older couple who appeared to be directing proceedings. John Devonshire looked at his new home with pride and felt contented with life. He saw that Mr and Mrs Perkins had already taken charge of the removals and made a mental note he had made the right decision when hiring them as housekeeper and gardener. James's mother had already opened the car door and was greeting the couple warmly.

"Ah, so this must be Young Master James," the woman said in an accent that James thought sounded 'country like' as she came forward to greet him with a warm, friendly smile. Just then her husband stepped forward and took James's hand in a strong grip, pumping it up and down so vigorously James thought his teeth would fall out.

"Pleasure to meet yeh Young Master," he said in the same country-like tones as his wife. "Hope I didn't hurt yeh – don't know me own strength sometimes," he added with a chuckle.

"This is Mr and Mrs Perkins," his father explained, "they will be looking after things for us in the house and garden."

"Don't yeh worry Mr Devonshire, sir, me and the missus will see to unloadin', 'tis all marked and then you and Mrs Devonshire can do the unpackin' later at your leisure like."

His mother was talking to Mrs Perkins who suggested they might like a cup of tea after their long journey.

"Kettles boiled," she said, "and I've got some lovely scones I baked this mornin' and there be home-made jam and cream too."

At the mention of food, James realised he was actually quite hungry and followed them all into the house and down the huge oak panelled hallway into the kitchen. They sat down at the large table in the middle of the room while Mrs Perkins brewed the tea in a big pot on the range and brought out a plate from the pantry, piled high with freshly baked scones.

"Tuck in Young Master. Looks like yeh need filling up wiv some good honest country food – we'll soon have them cheeks glowin' wiv' health."

James tucked in, the smell was irresistible and they tasted even better. He decided that he was going to like homely Mrs Perkins with her round pink cheeks and sparkling blue eyes. After three scones, James felt stuffed and his mother worried that he might feel sick.

"Don't yeh worry, Mrs Devonshire, ma'am, the young lad'll be just fine," she suggested she might like to see his room and start sorting out his things.

With that James followed his mother down the hallway and up the stairs, trying to avoid the increasing number of boxes that were piling up everywhere.

"We were not sure which of these two rooms you might prefer," said his mother opening the first door with a flourish. It was a fine room, large but not too big and overlooked the back of the house. There was a fireplace that would have been used to warm the occupants in the days before central heating but in spite of that James thought the room was cold and uninviting. In fact he had felt a distinct chill when he had stepped inside, although his mother seemed unaware.

"Can I see the other room?" he asked.

"Of course, dear, we want you to be happy here," his mother replied giving him a reassuring hug.

The other room was not quite so big and occupied the corner of the house with two windows, one looking out onto the back garden and a smaller one to the side with a window seat. There was no fireplace but that didn't bother James. It was plenty big enough for his things and he immediately felt comfortable, as though it had always been his room.

"I'd like his one, please, Mummy."

"Are you sure James, the other one is much bigger."

"I know but this one feels nicer, sort of cosy," James replied looking out of each window in turn.

From the larger window he could see the terrace bordered by flowerbeds and steps leading down to the lawns with woodland beyond. Sitting on the window seat looking out of the small side window the view was of a huge Cedar Tree.

'Gosh, that must be old,' thought James as it towered above the house. Making a mental note that he would explore it as soon as he could, James set about sorting his room. His bed had been placed so he could look out of the large window and Mrs Perkins was busy laying it with fresh clean linen. An alcove was set in the wall to the side of the small window and James decided that would be the perfect place for his books and favourite toys.

"There now," said Mrs Perkins smoothing the striped bed cover, "it looks like home already, Master James." With that, she hurried out of the room leaving him to continue arranging the shelves. It was sometime later that his mother breezed in to find him sat on the window seat looking as if he was a thousand miles away.

"James," she scolded, making him jump and almost fall off the seat, "you still haven't hung your clothes in the wardrobe and it will soon be time for Mr and Mrs Perkins to go home. Mrs Perkins has prepared dinner for us so you had better come down to eat now."

It was 8 o'clock the following morning when James awoke and for a moment wondered where he was. Rubbing the sleep from his eyes he climbed out of bed and drew back the heavy curtains. "Of course it's the new house," he said looking out of the window at the sun creeping across the lawn. Hurriedly he dressed and the smell of bacon, eggs and freshly baked bread drew him to the kitchen. Mrs Perkins was cooking breakfast on the range and his mother had begun unpacking boxes of her best china ready to display in the dining room.

"Good mornin', Master James – are yeh hungry?"

"Good morning, Mrs Perkins," replied James politely. "Yes, I am rather."

"Excellent," said his mother, "we'll sit down to breakfast the minute your father comes in."

The morning passed quickly, everyone busy unpacking boxes and finding new homes for all their possessions. James felt lonely with no one to talk to or play games with. He wandered outside to explore the gardens and particularly the huge Cedar Tree that he could see from his bedroom window. It dominated that side of the house and must be very old, thought James. As he stood looking up through the branches he wondered who had planted it and then became aware of the noisy rooks circling above. "You don't scare me," James shouted at them in false bravado. He hadn't seen rooks in London and wasn't sure if they were dangerous.

"Lord no, they's just noisy." Mr Perkins, who was tidying up empty boxes into the garage, laughed. "They've had rooks here since me grandfather's day and afore maybe. That's why 'tis called Rookery Manor. Have yeh ever climbed trees Master James?"

"We didn't have trees in our garden in London," replied James wistfully.

"Good Lord! A fine young lad like you ain't never climbed a tree! Well there be plenty here to choose from." Mr Perkins laughed waving his arms towards the woods. "Mind yeh go careful, don't want yeh fallin' down an breakin' sommat', yey Ma 'ould never forgive I. See yon Cedar Tree, that be easy to climb a little ways, not too high mind." with that Mr Perkins resumed carrying boxes into the garage.

James wandered back towards the Cedar Tree. He could see now that there were quite a few footholds to help one climb into the lower branches. Someone had carved initials into the trunk, the letters R.D. appeared twice, linked together by a curved line which curled around each set of initials. James touched the rough wood of the tree, tracing the letters with his finger. 'I wonder who R.D. was,' he thought. A sudden sharp tingle in his fingertips almost like a mild electric shock caused James to pull his hand away. "Ooh!" he exclaimed rubbing his fingers and then tentatively touching the letters again; this time there was no tingle. "It must have been some rough wood," James mused and dismissed it from his mind as he decided to try climbing the tree.

It wasn't too difficult to reach the lower branches just as Mr Perkins had said. Were one of the branches grew out of the trunk there was a small shallow curve as though it had been worn that way by countless generations of children who had climbed the Cedar Tree. James settled himself down and his body fitted in just perfectly. From his vantage point he could see Mr Perkins still busy at the garage and over to the far side lay the woods and beyond that farm fields stretched almost to the horizon. From the other side he could see the village of Stanton Seymour with its tall church spire. 'This will make a great hiding place,' thought James with a smile, 'I can see for miles and miles.'

Just then his thoughts were interrupted by the sound of his father's voice calling, "James, James where are you?" Not wishing either of his parents to know about his new den and anyway his mother would have a thousand fits if she knew he had climbed a tree, he stayed quiet until his father went searching elsewhere. Once the coast was clear he slowly climbed down – it was easier to go up than to come down he discovered.

"There you are, *where* on earth have you been James, didn't you hear me calling?"

"Sorry, no, Dad. I've just been exploring," James decided not to enlighten his father any further, pleased at his little secret.

Dark clouds appeared above the woods and a stiff breeze descended from nowhere. Mr Perkins lifted his eyes skywards. "There be a storm brewin' or my name's not Perkins." Leaning heavily on the spade he was using to tidy up the flower borders, he turned to James, who had decided to help out of sheer boredom. "Yeh mark my words it'll rain in a few minutes, a right downpour if I'm not mistaken. Best get back to the house afore yeh get soaked."

Sure enough the heavens opened and rain came down in a steady torrent just as James reached the kitchen door. Wandering from room to room it seemed everyone was too busy to notice him, still unpacking boxes and finding new homes for everything. James felt very lonely and thought about his friends back in London and wondered what they might be doing. Sitting in his room on the window seat he stared out at the Cedar Tree now being battered by the wind and rain, even the rooks had disappeared. A feeling of restlessness came over James and he found himself drawn out onto the landing. At the far end, past all the bedrooms was another door, which his mother had said, led up into an attic. Curiosity and something else, James couldn't quite put his finger on, led him down the corridor. When he turned the doorknob, the same sharp tingle he had felt when he touched the Cedar Tree made him cry out and draw his hand sharply back. Tentatively he reached out to touch the doorknob again – nothing. Just like before when he ran his fingers over the carved letters on the Cedar Tree. Strange, thought James, looking at his fingers carefully, but they looked the same, perfectly normal. He pushed the door, which was stiff as though no one had opened it for a long time. It creaked loudly, thankfully no one would hear it above the sound of the wind and rain, besides everyone was far too busy to bother about what he was doing. Pushing the door until the gap was wide enough to squeeze inside James searched for a light switch. A steep wooden staircase lay in front of him, dimly lit from the light bulb in the attic above. Cautiously he climbed the stairs, a mounting feeling of anticipation and excitement gripping hold of him. At the top a large attic room lay before him lit by a single light bulb although a small round window allowed in some daylight. However today, only dark storm clouds and rain could be seen through the windowpane. The room smelt dusty as though no one had used it for years, the window was dirty and hung with cobwebs. As his eyes became accustomed to the gloom James became aware of a large rocking horse at the far end near the window and beside it stood a small trunk. 'Wow' thought James 'I wonder who left that here.' Never having had a rocking horse, he couldn't resist trying it out, especially as it was very large and took him comfortably. Slowly, he began to rock back and forth. Closing his eyes, he began to imagine he was actually riding across the fields beyond the house, he could hear the pounding hooves and feel the wind on his face. It felt so real, there was a smell of new mown hay and bird song filled the air so that James quickly opened his eyes but yes, he was still in the attic sat on the rocking horse but it had felt so real, it was *very* strange.

Climbing down, he turned to the small trunk, it was locked but unlike the room was not covered in dust. Looking around for any signs of a key, he noticed the ribbon around the rocking horse's neck and hanging from it a small key. I wonder, thought James, carefully removing the ribbon. Sure enough it fitted the lock. Peering inside he could make out a collection of objects but his eyes were drawn to a red silk scarf. Lifting it out of the trunk he carefully unwrapped the scarf to reveal a small leather book with the initials R.D. in gold on the front. Opening the first page he was confronted by a riddle.

"If my secrets you would find
Read me not in a place confined
Seek the vast eternal sky
Where rooks and buzzards fly on by
To sit within a cloud of green
And find a world as yet unseen."

James read the words over and over again yet he still could not understand what they meant. Turning the pages, he realised it was a kind of diary written by a girl who had lived in Rookery Manor many, many years ago. Before he could begin reading his mother's voice could be heard calling him from somewhere below. Quickly wrapping the diary in the red silk scarf, he placed it back in the trunk – he would explore this another time. Briefly stroking the rocking horse he ran down the stairs, closing the door behind him. This place would be his secret.

Chapter 2 –
The Secret of the Diary

Lying in bed James stared at the ceiling, the summer holidays would soon be over and he would have to start a new school. He sighed heavily; it was not something he was looking forward to. Climbing out of bed he drew back the curtains. Outside the sky was blue with a few fluffy clouds like balls of cotton wool and the sun was already drying the lawn after yesterday's downpour. A fine mist was rising from the grass and James could see the ornamental pond was filled almost to overflowing. The sun glinted on the water and the whole garden took on an almost magical appearance. This morning he would return to the attic and see what else was there once breakfast was over.

Once again, he couldn't resist the temptation to climb on the rocking horse but today nothing exciting happened. Sitting on the floor James opened the small trunk, lifted out the red silk scarf and opened the diary. Although the sun streamed through the small round window it wasn't light enough to read the tiny handwriting properly. Wrapping the diary back in the red silk scarf James placed it in his pocket. Closing the door to the attic, he quietly went downstairs and out into the sunshine. The only place where no one would disturb him would be up in the Cedar Tree.

Pausing briefly to look at the carved initials, James realised they were the same as those on the diary. Curious, he ran his fingers over the initials and once again he felt that mild electric shock. Puzzled and not sure what to make of it, he looked up into the tree and quickly began to climb. Settling himself down into the hollow he took the silk scarf out of his pocket and carefully unwrapped the diary. It had been written by a young girl called Rebecca who had lived at Rookery Manor with her family many, many years before. She had even occupied the same bedroom James now slept in. 'I wonder what kind of a person she was' he mused 'and had *she* ever climbed the Cedar Tree?' It was a very hot August day with hardly a cloud in the sky and the rooks were particularly noisy. James rested the book on his lap and his mind began to wander, imagining the girl and what she might look like. He felt sleepy and his eyes began to close.

He awoke with a start. 'Gosh, I mustn't go to sleep, I might fall down,' he thought peering through the branches to see how far down it was. Rubbing his eyes James became aware of a strange, large bird sitting on the branch a few feet away. He rubbed his eyes again, thinking he was dreaming, but no, the bird was still there staring at him.

"It's definitely not a rook," James said aloud. It was bigger than anything he had ever seen before with a snowy white head and chest; its belly and shoulders were a reddish brown like a polished chestnut. Tentatively stretching out his hand to see if it *was* real, the bird suddenly threw back its head uttered a strangely haunting cry and with huge outstretched black wings it disappeared.

'I must definitely be dreaming,' thought James when children's voices drifted up from the ground below. What on earth were village children doing in his garden? Carefully holding tight to the tree so he didn't fall, James looked down through the branches to find a young girl looking up at him.

"Are you going to stay up there all day James," she chided, "or are you going to come down and play?"

'How does she know my name' he thought feeling a little confused, 'I've never seen her before in my life.'

Curiosity getting the better of him, James slowly climbed down. The young girl smiled at him with a warm and friendly smile (the kind that could melt even the hardest heart). His obvious confusion made her giggle and her eyes sparkled with mischief. She has the most beautiful eyes thought James, like the clear blue of the sky above. Mesmerised, he stared rooted to the spot, this made the girl laugh even more but not in an unkind way.

"Hello James, I am Rebecca but everyone calls me Becky."

"How do you know *my* name?" James sounded mystified.

"Mtumwa told us," she answered. "He brought you here," and she pointed to a large bird sat on a nearby fence. It was the very same bird he had seen up in the Cedar Tree moments before.

Then James realised he was no longer in the garden at Rookery Manor. All around him everything was strange and different, the air smelt hot and full of perfume, even the tree was no longer a Cedar Tree.

Becky's voice broke into his thoughts. "This is Rory, my brother," she said as a young boy stepped forward to shake James's hand. Rory was a little older than James, with blond hair and eyes of emerald green, but the same warm, friendly smile as his sister.

"I … I don't understand," James muttered feeling even more confused and a little nervous. "Where am I and how did I get here?"

"Where you are is easy," replied Rebecca, "you are in Africa at our home in Kenya but how you got here is more complicated. Come and sit in the garden and we'll try to explain."

The boy and girl then began a strange tale, which at first seemed to James unreal, as though it came straight out of a storybook. They had lived at Rookery Manor many, many years ago and Becky had been born there. She had always felt there was something special about the lovely old manor house as if it lived and breathed, watching over her but she had never felt afraid. Maybe that was why one day, hiding from Rory in the attic she discovered a diary just like James had found hers.

"So why did you leave?" enquired James.

Rory explained how their grandfather had moved to Kenya when he was 30 years old to work in the colonial administration offices in Nairobi. Eventually when he was 47, he built a tea plantation at Kericho to fulfil a long-held dream. His youngest son Philip, who was their father, was born in Kenya but both he and his brother when they were older returned to England. Then Grandfather Devereaux became too old and frail to run the plantation himself so their father inherited the business at the height of its prosperity and their parents moved them all to Kenya.

"I never wanted to leave Rookery Manor with its magic and the diary that transported us back in time once we discovered the key," said Becky.

"What's the key?" enquired James, his curiosity aroused once more.

"Well, the Cedar Tree is one of them." Replied Rory.

"Is it *magic* then?" asked James excitedly.

"Sort of, but it's Rookery Manor that holds the real magic," explained Becky. "The Cedar Tree is the bridge between your time and ours but nothing can happen without Rookery Manor. Mtumwa is your spirit guide and he is the one that transports you here but it can't happen without the diary."

"Is Prince still in the attic?" enquired Rory changing the subject.

"Who's Prince?"

"The rocking horse," he replied, "I use to ride him almost every day but now I ride *real* horses."

"He's very good too," said Becky admiringly. "Grandfather says he's a natural horseman."

"Oh yes, it's still there. I rode it myself and when I closed my eyes I felt as if I was really riding across the fields, I could almost feel the wind in my face."

Rory laughed. "That's the magic of Rookery Manor at work."

"Why did you leave him behind then?" asked James.

"Because he belongs to Rookery Manor and no one knows he's there. You see grown-ups can't see him, the house only reveals him to children," explained Rory.

James really wanted to learn more but he was conscious that he had been gone from home what seemed like a long time.

"I really must get back before I'm missed but how do I do that."   ˙

"Mtumwa will take you," Becky said, "but first you must climb back up into the Flame tree. Your parents won't even know you've been gone – time is different you see, hours here are like minutes in the future."

"Can I come and visit you again?" asked James, he really wanted to learn more about the magic of Rookery Manor and he felt sure the three of them could have great adventures together.

"Of course, but you must remember everything has to be in place or it won't work." Becky replied.

Just what she meant James wasn't sure but didn't give it any further thought. In the blink of an eye, he was back in the Cedar Tree and the rooks were squabbling in the branches above. He had little time to wonder whether he had dreamt the whole thing before he could hear his mother calling.

That night James couldn't sleep for wondering had it all *really* happened. Surely such magic didn't exist except in storybooks, so it must have been a dream. Determined to climb the Cedar Tree again tomorrow, he finally fell asleep to dream of rocking horses and strange large birds that carried him to another land.

The following morning James ran across the lawn towards the Cedar Tree flushed with excitement at the prospect of seeing his new found friends. Pausing to look at the carved initials, he suddenly knew who they belonged to. "Of course, Rory and Rebecca Devereaux." Now he was convinced it had been real, otherwise how would he know their names.

Climbing up into the hollow of the branch, he sat and waited for the bird to appear. He waited and waited but nothing happened. "Perhaps it was a dream after all," James felt disappointed, if it had been real, he could have had such wonderful adventures in Africa and he liked Becky and her brother Rory.

Feeling bored that afternoon he decided to explore the woods beyond their garden. It was cool under the canopy of trees as he followed a trail obviously made by animals. Maybe foxes, badgers or even the deer travelled these pathways when no one was around. The woods were strangely silent but James hardly noticed. His mind was occupied by thoughts of magic houses, trees, travelling through time and a girl called Rebecca. He sat down on a log to gather his thoughts — what had Becky said, something about 'everything being in place' what had she meant?

He tried to think back, what had he done the day before. As if a light bulb had been switched on in his head, James remembered the diary.

Not wishing to waste another minute, in his excitement James almost fell off the log he was sitting on. Turning around he realised he was not sure which way led home, lost in his thoughts he had not taken notice of where he had walked.

Looking around the clearing there were three paths leading off in different directions but which one would take him back to Rookery Manor? Aware that he was slightly lost, James decided to look for clues as to which path, he had walked down but none of them showed any footprints as the ground was too dry. The only sounds were the occasional rustling of leaves which made him feel uneasy as though someone was watching him. It had been warm and sunny when he first set off into the woods but now there was a distinct chill creeping into the air.

The sharp crack of breaking wood startled him. Quickly turning round, he came face to face with a young boy about his age. They stared at each other for what seemed minutes until the boy broke the silence.

"Yer not from 'round 'ere, are yeh?"

James thought the boy looked a bit scruffy. He had tousled blond hair, holes in his jeans with a dirty shirt hanging out of the back.

"I live at Rookery Manor," replied James in what he hoped was a superior sounding voice, not wishing to appear afraid.

"Yer lost then?" said the boy, unperturbed. James reluctantly had to admit he was.

"I knows these 'ere woods like the back 'o mi 'and. I come 'ere most days – it's peaceful. Come on then, I'll show yeh the way."

As they walked together James learnt the boy's name was Adam and he lived in the village with his parents. Like James he had no brothers or sisters but there the similarity ended. Adam's parents were simple country folk living in a small cottage on the edge of the village. His father worked on a nearby farm and was very proud of the vegetables he grew in their back garden. His mother cleaned the local doctor's surgery to earn a few extra pounds each week.

"Yer them new posh folk what just moved into the Manor 'ouse then?" enquired Adam.

It had never occurred to James that other people might look at his parents as 'posh'. He explained how they had come down from London to live in Stanton Seymour and how he hated leaving his friends behind.

"Ain't got many friends me 'self," said Adam wistfully, "just the birds and animals in Rookery Wood." His eyes lit up and a huge smile creased his face. "Yeh can be me friend James if yeh like but yeh must keep the secret of the woods and not tell a soul." Adam's voice became serious and a little threatening. "Can't 'ave everyone knowin' the secrets of the wood and scarin' all the animals away."

James wondered just what were the 'secrets of the wood' but had no time to ask as suddenly they were out in the sunshine and Rookery Manor lay in front of them.

"Come and meet my mum and dad," invited James to be polite.

"Ooh I ain't dressed for meetin' no posh folk, maybe another time." and with that Adam disappeared back into the wood as if the trees had swallowed him up.

It was now too late to climb the Cedar tree that would have to wait for another day. James smiled to himself; Adam wasn't the only one with a secret.

Chapter 3 –
The Girl in the Picture

The next few days passed in a haze of preparations for the new school where James was to board during the week coming home only at weekends and holidays – something he was not very sure about, never having been away from home before.

Now he would have to sleep in a dormitory full of other boys he didn't know, not in his own comfortable room at Rookery Manor where he felt safe. It was early September and as his father had pointed out he was too old to attend the local village school and besides he wanted his son to have the best education possible. John Devonshire had dreams for his son's future, great plans that James was, as yet, unaware of.

A new school is always a daunting prospect and for James it was no different. Meeting new teachers, making new friends and being away from home all would take some getting use too. Arriving early on the Monday morning he was shown around the school, his classroom, where he would sleep and keep his belongings. Luckily the other boys in his dormitory seemed nice enough and by the end of his first week James had begun to settle in and make a few friends. Before starting the new school there had been no opportunity to climb the Cedar Tree again so the first weekend home couldn't come quick enough, more than anything he wanted to see Rory and

Becky again to discover more about the magic of Rookery Manor and what was its purpose. His mother and father however, had other plans. They were all to travel up to London, his mother would be shopping and his father had an important business meeting. It had been arranged for James to spend the day with his old friends, which he would have been thrilled about a few weeks ago. Now, since his meeting Rory and Becky and discovering the thrill of travelling through time, the attraction was not quite the same and he couldn't hide his disappointment.

"I thought you would be pleased to see your old friends again," his father said a little annoyed.

"Yes, I am," replied James unconvincingly. "But I've been away at school *all* week and wanted to be home." The cross expression on his face echoed the deep disappointment he felt.

"Well, nothing can be done about it now, it's all been arranged."

Meeting his old friends again was fun but in those few weeks since they had moved James had changed in some way and he found them all a little childish and immature. His mind wandered to the Cedar Tree and its secret but he had no intention of telling them, they would probably laugh and think he was imagining things. It was late Sunday afternoon before they returned to Rookery Manor and there was no time to climb the Cedar Tree. As the light began to fade James looked wistfully out of his window and hoped the next week would pass quickly.

During the second week he began making a few more friends. Most of his teachers seemed nice and there were plenty of opportunities for sport and outdoor games but he still looked forward to the weekend. He was more fortunate than many who lived too far away to travel home except for term holidays. Eventually Friday dawned in a haze of fog and drizzling rain. James awoke with a feeling of excitement until he saw the weather outside his window. With a sinking heart he dressed and prepared for breakfast and lessons – tomorrow he convinced himself the sun would shine. At 4 o'clock his father was waiting for him in the lobby.

The drive home seemed to take forever, the air remained damp and it was still foggy but soon the welcome lights of Rookery Manor came into view, the front door opened and his mother was there to greet him with a kiss and a hug. Once inside the large hallway with its wood panelling, oak floor and thick red carpets he felt enveloped by the warmth as though the house itself had wrapped him in her arms. A familiar smell came from the kitchen and James hurried down the hall, flung open the door and stepped inside as homely Mrs Perkins laid the freshly baked scones on the table.

"Welcome 'ome, Master James," said Mrs Perkins with the same broad smile and twinkling eyes he had come to know. "I baked yer favourite, knowin' how hungry yeh are when yeh gets home. Will it be strawberry jam or the cherry?"

"Ooh, I'll have the strawberry please Mrs Perkins and lashings of cream too."

Mrs Perkins laughed. "This'll cheer yeh up an' no mistake with such an awful day out there."

James didn't need a second invitation but promptly tucked in, much to his mother's concern who chided him to leave room for his dinner.

The following morning James opened the curtains of his bedroom only to be greeted by a dull grey sky and pouring rain. He would not be able to climb the Cedar tree in this weather and the rain seemed in no mind to stop. Sitting on the window seat he applied his mind to the homework that needed to be handed in on Monday morning but his thoughts kept drifting away to Kenya, to Rory and Becky. He thought about the adventures they could have and wondered if they possessed the magic of Rookery Manor, if so, could he have magic too? Feeling frustrated he looked out of the window at the Cedar tree, perhaps tomorrow the rain would be gone. Should he go to the attic and ride Prince, but somehow that didn't seem exciting and anyway the attic would be dark and cold in this weather. He could explore the other contents of the trunk but for some unknown reason that too did not have any appeal.

Feeling bored he wandered out onto the landing. The bedroom next to his, which had felt so cold and uninviting the first time, had now been decorated as a guest room. Since that first time he had not set foot in there but a sense of curiosity made him reach out and turn the handle. Would the room still feel cold, he wondered. As he grasped the handle a sharp tingle of electricity made him cry out, the same tingle he had experienced before at the Cedar Tree and the attic. He couldn't help wondering why this happened, it was three times now, all very puzzling. The door swung silently open and James stepped inside. It looked very pretty now and more inviting with new furniture and decorations but there was still a strange feeling about the room that he couldn't quite put his finger on. He went to the window and looked out at the garden in the pouring rain, you couldn't see the Cedar tree from there but the woods lay beyond and he suddenly remembered Adam. After their meeting in the woods James had forgotten all about him what with the new school and everything. Adam was a strange boy and yet there was something likeable about him, they could probably be friends, that is if they ever met again.

Turning away from the window James noticed a picture on the wall opposite, 'I'm sure that wasn't there when I came in,' he thought. The painting was of a young, pretty girl sitting in a garden surrounded by birds and woodland animals. Looking more closely James recognised the garden of Rookery Manor, the flower borders were different but you could see the fish pond and in the distance a Cedar Tree. The girl in the picture looked about the same age as Becky but she had long golden hair and a very fair skin, whereas Becky's was burnt brown by the African sun. She looked delicate, fragile even, not like Becky at all. As he stared at her face James thought she closed her eyes momentarily and then smiled at him. "Can't have," he muttered to himself, "it's *only* a painting." This was weird. Deciding to ask his mother where the painting came from, James hurried out of the room and downstairs.

"A painting in the guest room, no dear you must have imagined it, there are no paintings there at all."

Puzzled he left her writing in the study while he went down the hallway to the kitchen. Mrs Perkins was busy preparing dinner before she and Mr Perkins, who was sitting having coffee at the table, were finished for the weekend.

"Why, Master James, yeh look like yeh seen a ghost," observed Mr Perkins, "white as a sheet yer are!"

"Am I? It's just that I thought I saw something but Mother says I'm imagining things."

"And what would that be Master James?" James then proceeded to tell Mr Perkins about the painting.

"Mmmm, strange," muttered Mr Perkins, "ain't never seen such a picture me'self but I do 'ear there are stories, 'ereabouts."

"What stories, do tell." James's curiosity aroused, he sat at the table eager to hear what Mr Perkins had to say.

"Now, don't yeh go fillin' the lads head with such daft nonsense," his wife scolded.

"Well, there are old folk around these parts what believes it."

"Oh, do tell Mr Perkins, I love a good story." James sat with his chin resting on his hands, eyes wide open in anticipation.

With that Mr Perkins began to describe the time when Rookery Manor was first built over three hundred years before, by a wealthy merchant who had an only child, a daughter called Emily.

"They said she 'ad strange powers. The animals came down from yon woods and she would talk to 'em and sometimes she knew about things afor they 'appened like." Mr Perkins paused.

"Oh, do go on Mr Perkins," James said eagerly, now wanted to know more.

"Well, the village folk back then thought she were a witch an would bring 'em bad luck, so some o' the men folk plotted to do away wiv'er."

"How did they do that?" said James now filled with curiosity.

"Tis said, they picked some poisonous mushrooms from yon woods which she ate and got ill. They called fer the village doctor but 'e could do nowt and she died. 'Er father vowed to avenge 'er death and bring the villagers responsible to justice, so one night they broke into the Manor 'ouse and 'ung 'im from yon Cedar tree. Some folk says 'er spirit 'aunts this 'ouse to this very day" – Mr Perkins nodded thoughtfully – "I ain't never 'eard of anyone *seein'* no ghosts 'ere though," he added as an afterthought.

"Course not. Stuff and nonsense, idle gossip," scolded Mrs Perkins.

"Do they say what she looked like?" enquired James.

"Aye, they say she were fair like them china cups o' yer Ma's – wiv long 'air like spun gold."

"But that's the girl in the picture," said James excitedly jumping up and down … "Come, come Mr Perkins come and see."

With that James pulled a reluctant Mr Perkins to his feet and led him to the guest room. Opening the door, Mr Perkins cautiously followed James inside.

"There on that waaa … all," James's voice trailed away because the wall was bare, there was *no* painting.

James looked puzzled but Mr Perkins felt relieved, all the same he did find it very strange, the young master not being one given to fanciful ideas. Returning to the kitchen he was confronted by his wife, obviously very cross. Hands on hips she laid into her husband with a tirade fit to stop even an elephant in its tracks.

"What possessed yeh, Albert Perkins, tellin' the lad such tales as will give 'im nightmares. Lord 'elp yeh if Mrs D should get to 'ere of it." Perkins looked sheepish, like a dog with its tail between its legs.

"I didn't mean no 'arm, 'tis only what folks 'ereabouts says. Sorry m'dear, that'll be the last of it."

James returned to his bedroom convinced that there was more to this story than maybe even Mr Perkins knew and he was determined to find out all he could about the girl who had lived at Rookery Manor centuries ago and her tragic death. Someone, somewhere must know something, probably Rory and Becky knew, after all they had told him about the magic of Rookery Manor and he vowed to find out the next time he climbed the Cedar Tree.

Much to his mother's dismay, James bolted down his breakfast Sunday morning, it was a glorious day and he was in a hurry to climb the Cedar Tree. Creeping up into the attic he took the ribbon from around the rocking horses' neck, carefully opened the trunk and lifted out the red silk scarf. Dropping its precious contents into his pocket he didn't even wait to lock the trunk behind him all thoughts were focused on the Cedar tree, traveling back in time to Kenya and seeing Rory and Becky again.

"I hope they haven't forgotten me," James said aloud as he climbed up into the lower branches.

The rooks were squabbling noisily above but he paid them no attention. Settling himself into the hollow and feeling excitement welling up from his shoes to envelop him like an invisible cloak, James carefully opened the diary and began to read. At first nothing happened and then a faint breeze ruffled his hair and caressed his cheek. A whoosh like the beating of huge wings and he knew that Mtumwa would be sat at the end of the branch. Steeling himself to look, he slowly lifted his eyes from the pages of the diary, sure enough Mtumwa was looking at him.

"It worked, it worked," muttered James excitedly. Should I say 'Hello' he wondered, looking into those dark piercing eyes as though expecting the bird to talk to him. They sat looking at each other and then, as before, James couldn't help reaching out to touch this strange, large bird. Once again, the huge wings opened, its head went back and uttered the same haunting cry before it disappeared. James instinctively knew he would have travelled with Mtumwa and now be in Rory and Becky's garden in Kenya.

Peering through the branches, he was surprised that the garden was empty no children's voices greeted him this time. Should he climb down or stay hidden and wait to see what happened. Before he could decide a girl's voice rang out from somewhere close by, calling his name. There she was, Becky, smiling up at him clearly pleased that he had returned.

"I'm so glad you found the way to return," she said, giving him a hug. "Rory has just gone riding," she added. "We could join him if you like."

"But I don't know how to ride, except for Prince the rocking horse."

"Don't worry." She laughed. "We can find you a quiet, safe horse to begin with."

They walked together around the house passed a profusion of flowering bushes the like of which James had never seen before. Butterflies and brilliantly coloured birds were everywhere; he would have liked to watch them but Becky had already turned the corner into the yard beyond. It was a large cobbled area with stables down one side and another with the tack rooms and stable boy's quarters. The yard was a hive of activity with horses being groomed and stables cleaned out.

"Hamisi." Becky waved at one of the men who seemed to be giving orders to a young boy. On seeing them his face broke into a huge smile, it was obvious he had a great affection for Rebecca. In fact, Hamisi, the chief stable boy (who was anything but a boy) had taught them both to ride almost from the time they had arrived in Kenya …

"Yes Miz Becky, what I do for you?" he enquired in a warm deep voice.

James found himself looking up into the friendly face of a tall dark Kenyan man whose brown eyes twinkled with delight at seeing them.

"We wish to go riding to find Rory but James has never ridden before."

"Aah, no matata Miz Becky, he can sit on Old General, I ain't never know him throw anyone off. He so slow, he meet himself comin' back." with that Hamisi broke into a deep laugh that brought tears to his eyes.

Old General, when he was brought out of the stable, turned out to be a grey gelding who had seen younger days but was still able to give a good steady ride. James eyed the horse with some trepidation – in his mind it towered above him.

As though reading his thoughts Hamisi said, "No matata Young Master, Miz Becky will look after you, she very good horse lady."

With that he hoisted James up into the saddle and Old General snorted but didn't move. Becky joined him on a beautiful chestnut mare whose coat shone like polished mahogany. They spent a few minutes teaching James how to hold the reins and command the horse, then she slowly walked them out of the yard and down a tree lined avenue. Beyond the trees James could see row after row of tea bushes extending far into the distance. Among the rows women worked picking the tea leaves and putting them into huge baskets on their backs. Eventually they turned away from the plantation and there in front of them lay a vast grassy plain dotted with the occasional copse of Acacia trees.

"There's a small waterhole over there," said Becky pointing to a distant stand of trees. "I bet Rory will be sat there watching in case any animals come to drink."

James was beginning to feel more confident and it was true, Old General seemed decidedly un-interested in moving very fast.

"Come on James, dig your heels into his side and we can go a little faster."

James obliged but Old General was not in the mood to move at a faster pace.

"Do it harder, you'll have to be firm. Show him who's Boss."

James tried again a couple of times and eventually Old General responded and broke into a slow trot. 'This is much better than riding a rocking horse,' he thought.

The trees grew closer and they could make out another horse standing quietly beside the waterhole. As they drew nearer the figure of a young boy could be seen sat on the ground next to the horse. Rory saw them coming and stood up to wave.

"So, James you found the way to visit us again."

"Yes, but it took me quite a while to figure it out."

"Well, it's great to see you," said Rory giving him a big slap on the back. "I didn't know you could ride?" he added with a grin on his face.

"He couldn't." Becky laughed. "That's why he's on Old General but I think he's actually done quite well."

"Must be a natural!" Rory's eyes twinkled and they all collapsed on the ground laughing.

It felt good and perfectly natural to be back with Rory and Becky, he only wished it could last. They lay on the ground looking up into a clear blue sky watching vultures circling high above. James was eager to learn more about the magic of Rookery Manor and he began by telling them about the girl in the picture.

"That will be Emily Beauregard — it was her father who built Rookery Manor and where the magic comes from," explained Rory who then went on to describe events much the same as Mr Perkins had. The one thing none of them knew was how or where the magic had started. Like James they had discovered the rocking horse and trunk in the attic but it was some time before the secret of its contents had been revealed to them, almost by accident. Even now they didn't know the meaning of all the items in the trunk except for the Peacock feathers and birds eggs they had left there. James had to admit he hadn't even looked beyond the diary.

"But why did the picture appear and then disappear?" James asked.

"It's through the picture that Emily appears to people but she never actually speaks. Her spirit lives in Rookery Manor and she uses the picture to communicate but we don't always know why, it's something of a mystery." Becky shook her head.

"Maybe *you* will discover the meaning of it all James," she added thoughtfully.

He was not really sure how. It was unlikely that Mr Perkins knew anymore and who else could he ask, he didn't know anyone from the village and they probably knew no more than Mr Perkins, it would just be local superstition. Then he remembered Adam, the scruffy boy he had met in the woods but surely, he wouldn't know anything. James realised they had been out for a long time and he must return to Rookery Manor before he was missed. Whispering into Becky's ear that he dare not stay longer, she understood and the three of them mounted their horses and rode back as fast as possible. Together they ran out of the stable yard towards the tall Flame Tree which stood in the garden.

"Now climb the tree and think of home, Mtumwa will come and take you back to your time."

James began to climb the tree when he remembered something important, he should have told her. Looking back, Becky had disappeared. 'There's no time to run after her,' he thought 'I must get home.' A sense of urgency gripped him, how on earth could he explain all this to his parents, they would never believe him. Mtumwa was already sat on the branch and before James could think twice he was back in the Cedar tree at Rookery Manor.

Lying in bed that night he couldn't sleep. He should have remembered to tell Becky he could not return for some time. He had started a new school and would only be home at weekends. Eventually he did fall into a restless sleep troubled by strange dreams he could not quite remember.

Chapter 4 –
Frosty Hollow

Some time passed by before James had a chance to think about Kenya but today, Saturday dawned clear and bright. His parents were both going out and would not be back until lunch time giving him the perfect opportunity to spend time with Rory and Becky. Mr and Mrs Perkins would just think he was playing around the garden or in the woods with Adam, they would be too busy to even miss him before his parents would be home.

As his father's car turned out of the drive, James hurried up into the attic, carefully opening the trunk he took out the diary. Downstairs Mrs Perkins was busy in the kitchen and with a cheery wave he said he was going to explore the woods but once out of sight he doubled back towards the Cedar tree. In no time at all Mtumwa was sat at the end of the branch, staring at him with those piercing eyes. Time travelling was strange thought James, because you felt nothing just a strong breeze and suddenly you were in a different place and time.

Climbing down he could see Mtumwa sat on the fence ruffling his white chest and preening the long glossy black wing feathers but there was no sign of Rory or Becky. Wondering what to do for the best James decided to walk around to the stable yard. Peering through the first door, it was empty just the lingering smell of horses and leather. The next two were also empty but as he came out into the yard, Hamisi walked around the corner, leading a horse that looked just like Old General.

"Why, you be that young friend of Miz. Becky's what rode Old General here," he said with a warm smile and a twinkle in his eyes.

"Yes, you remembered," replied James giving Old General's nose a pat.

"You be lookin' for the Young Masters?" enquired Hamisi. "They not here, gone to the coast, Mombasa way, with the Bwana and Mrs, not back for another week." James could hardly hide his disappointment.

"You travel long way?"

"Mmm, you could say that," volunteered James, knowing Hamisi would never believe him if he told the truth.

"Mebe you like say hello to Mzee, him lonely when family gone."

"Who's Mzee?" enquired James, wondering was it a bird, an animal or a person?

Hamisis smiled at James obvious confusion and explained Mzee was what they called Grandfather Devereaux, it meant 'Honourable Old Man' in Swahili and all the African workers referred to him by this title. Although Grandfather Devereaux built the tea plantation he was now too old to work and spent his days sitting in the sun with his memories and enjoying the company of his grandchildren.

"But I only know Rory and Becky."

James wasn't at all sure how he would explain his visit or where he had come from – their grandfather was bound to ask questions. In fact, none of them had ever given any thought as to an explanation of James's existence. It was something they must do soon if he was to meet their family in the future. Hamisi put Old General into one of the stables and closed the door.

"Mzee old man, he like company. Come, come." With that Hamisi took James by the hand and led him to a quiet part of the garden he had not seen before filled with a profusion of flowering bushes and trees not at all like anything he had seen in England. The air was filled with the scent of strange flowers and an array of beautiful butterflies flitted from blossom to blossom. A pathway wound itself from the terrace across the garden to a large arbour smothered in the flowers of a Bougainvillea. That *was* something James recognised but in England it only grew in Conservatories and would never reach the size of this one. Then he became aware of the old man sitting inside protected from the mid-day heat. His face was burnt brown by years of working under the African sun and had become dry and wrinkled with age but he had a warm and kindly face. Old now, Grandfather Devereaux's hair was white as snow – 'like the snows of Kilimanjaro' he would joke. Engrossed in reading he didn't hear them approach until Hamisi called out to him.

"Bwana Mzee, I bring you visitor."

The old man looked up from his paper and smiled. He didn't recognise the young boy who walked towards him but someone to talk too would be very nice.

"Well, young man and what's your name?"

"James, sir. I'm a friend of Rory and Becky."

"Ah, so you know my grandchildren," the old man paused for a moment. "They're not here you know, on holiday near Mombasa."

"Yes, I know, sir, Hamisi told me," James hoped he wouldn't ask where he came from or any other awkward questions.

"Come, sit down beside me." Grandfather Devereaux patted the seat beside him and suggested he might like a nice cool drink of mango juice. The problem now was how to avoid questions he couldn't answer, deciding the best way to solve this was by telling the old man all about his last visit and riding Old General. Grandfather Devereaux listened attentively and nodded from time to time but he was tired and before long the eyes had closed and his head rested on his chest.

James breathed a sigh of relief, quietly got to his feet and slipped away. Retracing his steps to find the stable yard, he was relieved that no one was there and continued around the house to the large Flame tree which would transport him back to Rookery Manor. Mtumwa was no longer sitting on the fence, in fact he was nowhere to be seen. A little anxious knot developed in the pit of his stomach, Becky had always been there before and he couldn't remember whether Mtumwa was as well. Climbing the tree he settled down feeling just a little bit nervous – what if it didn't work without either Becky or Mtumwa. He would be locked in the tree until they returned but that was not for another week. Telling himself not to panic but do as Becky always instructed 'think of home.' Closing his eyes and picturing Rookery Manor he waited for something to happen but there was no sudden breeze, no Mtumwa to take him home.

"I *must* get home; I *can't* stay here forever."

It felt as if a thousand butterflies filled his stomach and his heart began to pound in his chest. I must concentrate he told himself, I must think harder. He began to picture the Cedar tree, his warm, cosy room, the attic with Prince the rocking horse and finally the picture of a young girl called Emily filled his thoughts. At that moment something touched his face softly and a cool breeze enveloped him. Sighing deeply with relief, James opened his eyes and knew he was safe back in the Cedar tree.

That night he slept fitfully, dreaming of some faraway place where he was imprisoned forever with no way to get home. Through a haze he could see a fair-haired girl with blue eyes beckoning him to follow but when he stretched out his hand she disappeared. James woke with a start and a sudden feeling of panic for a few seconds until he realised this was his bedroom and he was lying in his own bed. Pulling the covers up to his chin he took comfort from their familiar warmth, feeling reluctant to make any move towards getting up. Through the curtains the early morning light was creeping across the sky and soon the house would come to life.

There was no point in climbing the Cedar Tree today as Rory and Becky would not be there. The day seemed to stretch endlessly and the disappointment at not seeing his friends and the fear he had felt when trying to get home had left James in a strange mood. There were no friends to distract him with silly games and there was no one special to talk too, he didn't know any of the village children except Adam – why had he forgotten all about Adam? Maybe he might have heard Mr Perkins story and just *maybe* he could tell James about the girl in the picture. At this prospect, James became excited and determined to meet up with Adam that day. The only problem was he didn't know exactly where Adam lived. Hadn't Mrs Perkins said he spent most of his time wandering the fields and Rookery Woods – that was where he would look for him. Decision made; James set off for the woods as soon as breakfast was over.

It was a lovely crisp, autumn morning and the sun was shining from a clear blue sky, this was surely the sort of day when Adam would be out and about. He decided to skirt around the outside of the woods first, after all it was still early and Adam might be in one of the fields, however, there was no sign of him. Retracing his steps until he came upon one of the many pathways which appeared well trodden as though regularly used, James wondered if Adam came that way as it was quite close to the village. Remembering how he had got lost the first time, James had brought a small penknife with him to make a mark on the trees to help guide him back. Every so often he paused to mark a tree and call Adam's name. The woods were cool and the ground covered in leaves that crunched under his feet. The sun filtered through the lacework canopy in shades of gold and russet brown, soon the branches would be bare and the woods would take on a less welcoming appearance but for now James was happy. Once again, he paused and called Adam's name, this time a voice answered from some way ahead. Peering out from behind a tree, a boy with tousled blond hair – he had found Adam.

A little shyly, the boys exchanged greetings and James used his new school as the reason for not meeting up with Adam before. It didn't take long for both boys to be laughing together as though they had always been friends. Eventually the path opened up into a small sunlit clearing and James suggested they sit down a while; he was anxious to ask Adam about the girl in the picture. He began by telling him about Mr

Perkins story and the merchants daughter Emily, who died so tragically.

"Oh yeah," said Adam. "I've 'eard them stories too, local superstition in'it," he then looked around furtively as though making sure no – one could overhear. Gripping James hand tightly, his face became serious.

"What I'm gonna tell yeh, yeh mustn't tell a livin' soul – specially not grown-ups."

Once more Adam checked that they were not overheard and then made James swear an oath that he would *not* repeat a single word to anyone. His version of events was almost the same as Mr Perkins, even to confirming the delicate, almost fragile appearance of the girl, Emily. Adam however, believed it *was* true that her spirit still lived at Rookery Manor. James then told him about the picture which had disappeared when he took Mr Perkins to see it and how the girl was exactly as they had both described.

"See, like I al'as said she still lives in the Manor 'ouse – she's livin' in that picture i'nt she?" Adam flushed with triumph as he had been proved right all along, then he became serious again.

"I'm goin' to trust yeh wiv mi secret." Adam pursed his lips and nodded as though convincing himself it was OK … "She comes to the woods, I seen her talkin' to animals in her special place," he paused thoughtfully. "Sittin' in the moonlight she looks like an angel."

James could contain his curiosity no longer and wanted to know where this special place was. Adam took a deep breath and looked thoughtful, slowly nodding his head he decided James could be trusted with the rest of the secret.

"Come on, I'll show yeh."

With that the two boys set off deeper into the woods. The ground began to slope downwards and the trees appeared taller. James was sure he would never find this place on his own but Adam strode confidently ahead, he certainly knew where he was going.

"This is Frosty 'ollow," Adam's voice interrupted his thoughts. "When all them leaves 'ave gone and winter frost nips bare branches it's proper magical."

James could imagine how it would look once all the leaves had fallen with just a canopy of bare branches curving overhead creating a long tunnel that would surely sparkle in the frost. The banks on either side were lush with ferns and moss-covered rocks, the silence broken only by fallen leaves crunching beneath their feet making a tapestry, a patchwork quilt that covered the ground. This part of the woods had a distinct atmosphere of its own, different in some way to the rest. As they walked deeper along the path, a pale light filtered down through the trees and a lingering mist rose before disappearing in the warmth of the sun as it moved across the sky far above.

"We're almost there," once again Adams voice broke into his thoughts.

The path had opened up into a clearing, a woodland glade where the sunlight felt warm on their faces. A small pool of water glistened in the centre and their voices disturbed a deer that was drinking. Within seconds it disappeared into the dense greenery as though it had never existed. Beyond the pool, a small rocky cliff festooned with ferns and ivy rose before them, water dripped down from a fissure creating a boggy area that eventually fed into the pool.

"See them two flat rocks, that's where she sits and behind them bushes there's a cave. Come on I'll show yeh." Adam's voice became excited.

With that he stepped forward and pushed aside the branches and brambles. James cautiously followed and sure enough there was a small opening in the rocks, big enough for Adam to slip through. His voice echoed from within as he called James to follow. Inside was cool and dark, just a little light entered to show the cave was not very big. At the entrance the boys could stand up but towards the back it narrowed and disappeared into the gloom.

"Have you ever been further inside?" enquired James.

"Naw, 'tis too dark," replied Adam, trying not to show he was afraid of going any further. "prob'ly full o' bats."

With his thoughts returning to the girl, James wanted to know more about what happened, how and when she appeared and did Adam hide in the cave? He explained it was usually on still, warm evenings when the moon was bright and he would hide behind the trees so not to be seen. He had to remain very quiet and not make a sound, if he did the girl disappeared in a puff of smoke.

"Why does she come here?" enquired James.

"Dunno," replied Adam shrugging his shoulders, "she al'as looks sad, troubled like, 'til the animals and birds come, then she talks to 'em."

"People say you do that." James butted in.

"Naw," replied Adam with a laugh, "there not afraid o' me but I can't talk to 'em."

The two boys went back through the narrow opening into the sunlight to sit on the flat rocks. James was still full of questions but Adam seemed reluctant to say anymore, although he did venture the information that village people rarely came to the woods because they thought it was haunted. Some even claimed to have seen strange things and in the past people were said to have disappeared and were never seen again.

"Well, I suppose it is in a way – haunted I mean," mused James, to which Adam nodded in agreement.

So far James had not mentioned anything about Rory, Becky or the diary. Maybe he would tell him soon but for now his mind was filled with those unanswered questions. How had the magic begun and what was its purpose? Even Rory and Becky hadn't discovered the secret of Emily's appearance in the picture and how the magic had continued even when they left for Africa? How many other children had experienced the magic of Rookery Manor and what was Adam's part in all of this, after all he had never even lived in the manor house. The two boys sat silently for some time each lost in his own thoughts. Suddenly Adam jumped to his feet.

"Ma'll have dinner on the table, should be gettin' back."

James realised he too was feeling hungry and they set off back through the woods with a promise to meet up again the following weekend.

That afternoon James once again felt compelled to visit the attic. Patting the rocking horse, he wondered how many children had ridden it over the years and who it had originally belonged to? Maybe the trunk would hold some clues. Taking the key from around Prince's neck he opened the clasp and bent down to search the contents lying beneath the diary wrapped in the red silk scarf. Placing them carefully on the attic floor beside him, he first took out some beautiful peacock feathers and a small delicate bird's egg, bluish green with speckles. These are the things Becky said they had put in the trunk, thought James. There was a small box and inside, perfectly preserved as though he had just found them, was a colourful butterfly and some dragonflies with wings as translucent and iridescent as an angel. He remembered Adam's description of Emily 'like an angel in the moonlight'. His thoughts dwelt on the picture he had seen of Emily and wondered how many of these objects had belonged to her? Had others also put special things in the trunk and if so why? James lifted out a tiny ball of golden yellow silk thread, a compass and a whistle. Was there a special meaning to all these items and if so, what was it or were they just mementos from other children who had lived at Rookery Manor in the past?

Returning to the task in hand he next lifted out a beautifully embroidered silk purse, inside he discovered a number of old coins and next to it a pair of dainty soft kid gloves and a fan. As it fell open, he saw that each parchment section was decorated in exotic oriental birds and flowers. Perhaps it had come from the Far East, China or Japan maybe, then James remembered Emily's father had been a wealthy merchant. Could he have travelled to one of these countries and brought them back for her? As if to answer his curiosity a gold locket dropped to the floor from inside one of the gloves. Picking it up to examine more closely, James could see the fine engraving and the name Emily jumped out at him. Within the locket lay a strand of golden yellow hair, fine like gossamer – of course the girl in the picture had fine blond hair. The realisation that he was holding in his hand a part of Emily that had survived for hundreds of years gave him goose bumps – these things at least had belonged to her.

James had almost emptied the small trunk, all that remained were some shells, a strange piece of rock and a book of pressed flowers. Carefully turning the pages, he recognised some of the meadow flowers, poppies, buttercups, clover and scarlet pimpernel all perfectly preserved as if they had just been picked. On each page was written the flowers name, where, when and why it had been picked. Sometimes the notes were of a more personal nature, like a diary of how the person was feeling at the time. He felt almost certain whose book it was but just to make sure he turned the last page and read the words: 'This book belongs to Emily Beauregard, August 1716.'

The shells were just the kind you could pick up on any seashore but his attention was drawn to the strange piece of rock. Turning it over in his hands, it was like nothing he had ever seen before. It glinted when caught by the light as though flecked with pieces of metal. As James stared, he fancied it started to glow and it felt warm to the touch. Suddenly he gasped, dropping the rock which had become white hot in his hand. Looking down at his palms they were normal, yet it had felt as though they were being burnt. Gingerly reaching out to touch the rock again it now felt icy cold – what kind of rock was it, *where* had it come from? Unable to answer these questions James decided he would take it to school to see if his geography teacher could identify it. Wrapping it carefully in his handkerchief, he popped it into his pocket and began replacing other items back into the trunk. After making sure the trunk was securely locked, he put the key back around Prince's neck and went downstairs.

Chapter 5 –
The White Witchdoctor

For once, Monday morning and school couldn't come quick enough but James had to wait until the end of the afternoon in order to seek out Mr Wakefield the geography teacher who was sat marking papers in his classroom.

"Excuse me, sir, I wondered if you could identify this piece of rock for me."

Mr Wakefield looked up from his desk, removed his glasses and took the rock from James outstretched hand. "Mmmm." was all he said turning the rock over and over then replacing his glasses to look more closely. James waited for it to burn his hands too but nothing happened.

"Well, young man, where *exactly* did you say you found it?"

Knowing he hadn't mentioned anything about that, James mumbled something about finding it near his home – he wasn't about to reveal its true location to anyone.

"Mmm," said Mr Wakefield again as though contemplating his reply. "Well young man, I can't be certain but I would say it had fallen off a meteorite as it disintegrated on entering the earth's atmosphere. If you wish I can have it looked at more closely in the school's laboratory." Mr Wakefield peered at James over the top of his glasses.

James declined the offer saying it wasn't really that important and hurriedly left after thanking Mr Wakefield, who promptly returned to marking papers. However, his teacher couldn't help being more than a little curious as to how it had come into James's possession.

"Gosh a meteorite from outer space." It seemed impossible, had Emily found it or someone else and where? The mystery deepened and James determined to find out more somehow. The next time he visited Rory and Becky, he would ask them about it. He was also troubled by the fact that Mr Wakefield's hands had not been affected when he held the rock. Returning to the dormitory James carefully placed the rock at the back of his bedside locker, he needed to make sure no one else found it until he could safely take it back home.

The week seemed never ending but finally Friday came and he was on his way home again, this time for half term. Apart from the thought of enjoying Mrs Perkins scones and being in his own room it was the prospect of seeing Rory and Becky that filled him with excitement and he had also promised to catch up with Adam.

Pulling back the curtains' next morning James was relieved to see it was a clear autumn day. Eager to climb the Cedar Tree he hurriedly got dressed and went down to breakfast. Mr and Mrs Perkins were chatting in the kitchen while she laid the table and the smell of bacon and fried bread filled the air making James feel very hungry indeed.

"Well Young Master, 'tis nice to see yeh again," said Mr Perkins with a cheery grin, "the old place seems mighty quiet when yeh's not 'ere."

"Will yeh be wanting eggs with your bacon Master James?" his wife enquired as she busied herself at the range that occupied a large alcove along one wall of the kitchen.

"No thanks Mrs P just some toast and jam." The smell *was* good but he was in too much of a hurry to sit down.

"Dear me, that be no breakfast for a growin' lad like yerself," she scolded but her eyes twinkled as she looked at him.

"Ah he'll be home when his belly complains," said her husband with a laugh giving James a wink.

Not wishing to wait for his parents to come down he told Mrs Perkins to let them know he'd gone exploring and not to worry.

"Yeh'll be off to yon woods then." Mr Perkins called after him but James just waved as he ran out into the garden, letting them all think he had gone to the woods suited him fine. Once out of sight he climbed the Cedar Tree taking the diary out of his pocket where he had placed it the night before when he had returned the strange rock to the trunk. With a deep breath he turned the pages and began to read, a sudden whoosh and Mtumwa was waiting for him.

In the blink of an eye James was standing in the garden of Rory and Becky with Mtumwa sat on the fence as though he had always been there. Moments later and he heard Becky's excited voice.

"James, James you're here again, it has been so … ooh long, we missed you." Behind her stood Rory hands on hips and a big grin stretching from ear to ear.

"Great to see you James," he said giving him a brotherly slap on the back. "Sorry we were not here the last time you came but I guess you managed to get back home OK."

James then filled them in with the events of his previous visit and they all agreed it was a good idea to form a plan so he would know when they would not be at Kericho Plantation. He would come mostly at weekends and they would tell him in advance when the family would not be home. Before telling them all about the trunk and its contents James wondered how they knew about his last visit, had Grandfather Devereaux told them?

"Mtumwa came and told us," replied Becky. "We sent him back so you could get home safely."

"But I thought he just lived here in your garden; how did he travel to Mombasa so quickly?"

Becky glanced at Rory with a questioning look in her eyes – he nodded, "I guess we can let James into our secret now. The magic that allows Mtumwa to bring you here James also works in Kenya."

Sitting down in the shade of the Flame Tree they began a strange and mysterious tale. Not long after they arrived in Kenya their father took them on a trip into the bush to see the beauty and excitement of wild Africa and a chance encounter started them on a journey of discovery. During a bush walk with their father and an armed guide the sound of a distressed animal came from nearby. Their guide signalled them to remain quiet and not move while he went to investigate. They discovered a female cheetah caught in a trap and beside her sat a tiny cub, whimpering and shivering with cold. Sadly, they could not save the mother but took the cub back to their camp and subsequently home to the plantation where she survived, becoming very tame. They named her Honey because as Rory said she was the colour of sweet honey and was now considered a member of the family. This was to be the beginning of their new life rescuing a variety of injured creatures, many of whom still lived in or around the plantation. One day during this time Mtumwa arrived and at first, they thought he was just resting in their garden but when days later he was still there and appeared reluctant to leave they became curious thinking maybe he was injured.

Rory, being slightly braver, reached out to touch the Fish Eagle and instantly they had the same experience as James when he first saw Mtumwa in the Cedar Tree. However, they found themselves in a forest clearing with a thatched hut and sitting beside a fire a small old man speaking softly in a strange language to the Fish Eagle. He turned to look at them and smiled, beckoning them forward. Although his features were African, the man's skin was pale white and he had curly grey hair.

"He was an Albino," interrupted Becky, "rather unusual in Africa." She went on to explain the old man was a white Mganga or witch doctor and because of his colour was regarded by the local people as sacred and possessing very powerful magic. It was he who had summoned them and sent Mtumwa. Through his powers he had seen their ability to communicate with the wild creatures and knew they had been touched by magic; he had called them "Children of the Chosen". The magic that Emily had bestowed travelled with them to Kenya long enough for the Mganga to recognise it and call them to him.

"In Africa there are many Mganga who practice black magic and the people fear them but Mchawi only uses his powers for good and to protect the Sacred Mountain," said Rory exchanging glances with his sister and then added, "I think we can entrust our secret to you James, after all you have been touched by Emily's magic too." Becky nodded in agreement.

James was eager to learn about the Sacred Mountain, where was it, what made it sacred and why had they been called 'Children of the Chosen'?

"We will take you there but not today. First you need to know about Mtumwa and Mchawi the white Mganga." It was he who told them that some children are chosen to receive special powers to use for good.

"Chosen by whom?" enquired James.

"We don't really know yet," replied Rory, taking a deep breath he continued. The white witchdoctor lived in a forest at the foot of the Sacred Mountain in the north west of Kenya and had always possessed strange powers, much like Emily Beauregard. One day while walking through the forest he found a baby Fish Eagle on the ground; it had fallen from the nest high above and broken its wing. Without Mchawi's help it would certainly have died, so he carried it back to his hut and gradually over the days that followed, it became stronger and its wing healed. He named the bird Mtumwa, which means Messenger and once it reached adulthood, Mchawi imbued it with magical powers.

"Sometimes Mtumwa disappears for days because he has returned home to the Sacred Mountain," interrupted Becky, "but he always comes to us when we need him."

James wanted to know how Emily and Rookery Manor fitted in but neither of his friends knew the answer. It seemed as if, once you had been touched by magic, then no matter where in the world you were, it would find you but to what purpose still had to be revealed.

By the time they finished their tale James had almost forgotten his news – he was learning how many mysterious and magical things there were. When he lived in London such things existed only in story books or so he had thought and yet here he was living with magic. James began by telling them about the picture, Adam's secret and the contents of the trunk. When his new friends had lived at Rookery Manor, Adam, like James hadn't been born, neither had they known about Frosty Hollow, the hidden cave and Emily's appearance there. Becky explained it had been to her Emily first revealed herself in the picture in much the same way as James had experienced.

"She will appear to you again from time to time, usually when something important is about to happen."

James was now eager to discuss the contents of the trunk in the attic. Listing all the various objects he had uncovered it became obvious that not all had existed during Rory and Becky's time, nor had they discovered any special meanings. Some of the things must have belonged to Emily and they presumed other items had been placed there by children like themselves.

"Well, if that's the case, why is yours the only diary there?" queried James.

Rory explained how at a time decided by Emily, James would probably be instructed to begin writing a diary just as Becky had been and when he left Rookery Manor forever, then, just like Becky, he must leave it in the trunk. Once that happens, her diary will disappear as though it never existed and contact between them will no longer be possible. Only the diary of the last child to live in the house who has been touched by the magic ever remains until it is found and the cycle can begin again.

"But does that mean one day I will not be able to see you both again?"

"Only if you leave Rookery Manor, then the spell that connects us will be broken," said Becky.

James felt disheartened by the thought and it must have shown on his face as Becky put her arm around his shoulder and assured him it wouldn't happen for a long time. Turning his attention back to the contents of the trunk he asked about the locket, the whistle and compass and lastly the strange piece of rock. Rory shook his head and said they had never seen them except for the whistle.

"This is to summon your spirit guide if you are in danger or serious trouble," he explained, "but you cannot use it more than four times before it disappears forever so think carefully James before you use it," he warned. "You will hear nothing but don't be tempted to blow it again or you will use up all four times at once. The most important thing is that Mtumwa will hear it and come to your rescue."

"So should I carry it with me always?"

"No, no need. All you do is clap your hands four times and say 'come whistle' and it will appear."

Becky suggested that Emily must have put those objects there and perhaps she would reveal a special secret, sometime in the future, meant only for him. James was no nearer understanding the meaning of the trunks contents and yet he was convinced they had to be there for a purpose. Maybe the answer lay back in Rookery Manor and not in Kenya after all. Becky's voice broke into his thoughts.

"We have something special to show you."

Coming towards them was Honey the cheetah closely followed by a small gazelle with only three legs.

"Father couldn't save its leg but she is fine now. Honey looked after her and now they are inseparable." Becky stroked the cheetah lovingly and Honey responded with a soft purring sound just like a cat.

"We've called the gazelle Tommy and hope it will become as tame as Honey one day. It's still a little bit afraid but we can never send it back to the wild, with only three legs it just wouldn't survive."

It amazed James that wild animals could become so tame, seemingly Emily must have passed on these powers to his friends. I wonder if she will do the same for me, he mused, after all Becky seemed certain that Emily would appear to him again. Bringing his thoughts back to the present James was still puzzled as to why he could travel back in time to Africa, what was the reason and why did the white Mganga contact Rory and Becky and call them 'Children of the Chosen'? He was sure the three of them could have great adventures together but surely the magic didn't happen just for fun and what part did Emily play in all of this?

Chapter 6 –
The Sacred Mountain

Due to the half-term holidays, there was no school for more than a week so James had arranged to return in a couple of days when his friends would take him to the Sacred Mountain.

Hoping to learn more, he once again took all the objects out of the trunk, looking at each one carefully but nothing happened. All he knew for certain was the whistle was to be used in case of great danger to summon Mtumwa, Becky's diary was his passport to travel through time and the book with pressed flowers had belonged to Emily. On a piece of paper James listed all the items with a space to write down a possible meaning – at least it was a start. With his thoughts centred on Emily he decided to see if the picture appeared again. Carefully putting all the items back inside the trunk, he locked it and returned the key to Princes neck. Patting the rocking horse, he promised to ride him again soon.

Opening the door to the guest room he was disappointed to find nothing unusual apart from the chill he always felt in the air. Looking hopefully at the wall he wished something would appear but today as so many times before it remained blank. Feeling deflated James went to the window and looked out at the garden which was changing now that summer was over, the leaves were turning to autumn shades and preparing for winter. He found the thought of the long winter ahead depressing, the cold and wet, only the prospect of spending time with Rory and Becky lifted his spirits. Remembering he was to see them again the next day, changed his mood and a feeling of excitement knowing he would visit the Sacred Mountain and his journey of discovery would hopefully take him nearer to understanding the connection between them all.

Before sleeping that night he crept into the attic and took the precious diary from the trunk, slipping it into his pocket for safe keeping. Next morning, once he was left to his own devices, James climbed the now familiar Cedar Tree. It had become like an old and trusted friend, an important part of his life, just as he couldn't imagine life without it or Mtumwa. Almost before he knew, the familiar voices of Rory and Becky filtered up through the branches of the Flame Tree and he was climbing down into their garden.

"Today is a very special day," said Rory, "because many new and secret things will be revealed to you. The first time you meet the white Mganga remember he is a magic Holyman with many powers we don't understand." James nodded.

"Come on," said Becky, "we must ride to the waterhole, the same one you rode to on Old General."

How could I ever forget that thought James as it had left him with a sore bottom he couldn't explain to his mother. Together they set off towards the waterhole this time with James holding tightly onto Rory as speed and secrecy were of the utmost importance. Becky had explained it was necessary that no one should see where they went. On reaching the trees they dismounted and tied the horses so they couldn't stray. Rory looked around carefully to make sure they were alone and then he took out of his pocket what looked like a handful of seeds which he proceeded to throw up into the air were they exploded into a cloud of dust. As they fell to the ground the air became filled with a strange perfume and then the sound of huge wings beating back and forth.

"Quickly, we must form a circle and hold hands," called Rory.

Mtumwa hovered above them and as he lowered his talons the three friends raised their hands together as though to touch him. In an instant the same feeling James experienced in the Cedar Tree enveloped them. When he opened his eyes, they were still holding hands but standing in a forest of huge trees that towered above him the like of which he had never seen before.

"Come on, let's not waste any more time," said Rory marching off down a track as though he knew exactly where he was going. Becky and James hurried after him but James couldn't help stopping to look at the monkey's swinging from branch to branch as though they were following them … The call and chatter of strange birds was all around but his two friends seemed not to notice. The gloom of the forest gradually gave way to bright sunlight and James found himself in another much larger clearing. On the far side was a thatched hut with a curl of grey smoke rising from a fire in the front. Beside the fire sat the crouched figure of an old man with African features but his skin was almost white and he had long curly grey hair. He was naked except for a loin cloth and around his neck a thin rope hung with a variety of small bones and shells. Mtumwa sat preening himself nearby and the old man was talking to him softly in a language James had never heard before. On seeing the children, the old man stood up and smiled broadly with outstretched hands. Both Rory and

Becky bowed respectfully and clasping their hands he greeted them warmly. They introduced James, who was not at all sure what to do or say but Mchawi smiled and shook his hand.

"So, my young friends you are here to seek Mchawi's help I think?" and continuing to hold James's hand he added, "Your friend, I feel has also been chosen but for a different purpose I sense."

"Mchawi," Becky spoke up, "we have spoken to James about the Sacred Mountain and promised him an explanation because he has come from the future and now lives at Rookery Manor just like we did."

"Aaah, but his destiny does not lie with us my children," the old man voice was serious. "He will help you when he visits and we can enlighten him as to many things but the magic requires something different of him."

Their curiosity was aroused even more and the need for answers filled their thoughts. Mchawi bade them be patient while he disappeared into the hut and returned with a large bowl, placing it on the fire. From the pouch around his waist, he took what looked like dust and threw it into the bowl, immediately it crackled and burst into flames. The children watched in silence as the old man started to chant and wave his hands in the air. Slowly a white mist began to rise from the bowl, at first it appeared to circle Mchawi, around and around it went until finally settling above the bowl like a huge white cloud. The old man continued to chant and dance around the fire as it crackled and spat, throwing burning embers onto the ground. The cloud appeared to bubble like boiling water and slowly a face began to appear. At the same time the three of them murmured the words 'Emily' and turned to look at each other in amazement. As the cloud dispersed the face that was left behind was unmistakeably that of Emily Beauregard. But how had Mchawi conjured up *her* face, it was hardly possible that he knew her? Meanwhile the white Mganga had collapsed in a heap on the ground, the effort required to create such magic had drained him of all energy.

"Did you see what you came for my young friends?" he asked in a hushed voice.

"But we don't understand Mchawi. Where did the face of the girl come from?" Becky looked puzzled as did the two boys.

Mchawi had now got to his feet and sat down beside the fire.

"As I told you, your young friend has a different destiny to you both my children. The magic brought me the face of a young girl who has touched you all but for a different reason," the old man turned his attention to Rory and Becky. "I only know the purpose for which you both were called to me, as for your friend, he was sent here to learn in order to fulfil that for which the girl has chosen him."

The three children looked at each other more puzzled than ever for it seemed as if Mchawi was talking in riddles. Sensing their confusion, he added, "All will be revealed in the fullness of time – we must be patient."

At that moment a small grey monkey with a black face climbed up onto Mchawi's shoulder and appeared to whisper in his ear.

"Ah, yes Ziwadi, our guests wish to see the Sacred Mountain and learn its secrets and we must offer them some cool water to drink, they have come a long way."

The monkey continued to chatter excitedly into Mchawi's ear and James noticed she had lost one hand. The old man stroked her head and seeing James's expression he spoke again.

"My little Ziwadi." He looked at her tenderly. "She lost her hand when she was a tiny baby. Her mother was a low-ranking member of their troop and during a jealous fight with another female her tiny hand was bitten off. She came to me for comfort and has been with me ever since – she is my gift." Mchawi smiled at the monkey who responded by poking a finger in his ear which made the three friends laugh so much tears ran down their cheeks.

"But James, we have to show you the Sacred Mountain and that which it guards. Come Ziwadi, let us go."

As they all walked deeper into the forest Mchawi began to explain how local tribes regard these forests as sacred places and the dwellings of their ancestors.

"There are abandoned villages in these forests, built centuries ago which contain the graves of those who lived there. It is a sacred duty to care for these places and I, the Mganga Nyeupe, am entrusted to watch over them." He paused for a moment, resting his old body on his stick with Ziwadi still chattering in his ear.

James was curious to find out where they were going but he couldn't help looking around there were so many new things to see. High above in the trees monkeys swung effortlessly from branch to branch and the air was filled with the humming of unseen insects. Occasionally he would get a fleeting glimpse of deer and yet they were not at all like the Roe deer in Rookery Woods.

"They're called Bongo," said Becky sensing his curiosity. "They live only in dense mountain forests and those big black and white monkeys with the long bushy tail are called

Colobus. Some people kill them for their tail and that lovely white mantle down their back."

"That's terrible," said James shocked at the thought that people could be so cruel. He realised they had now begun to walk up hill and the forest was no longer so thick with lush vegetation.

"We are almost there," said Mchawi slightly out of breath as he was no longer a young man.

The forest opened up into a huge clearing and beyond, the mountain rose up in front of them. The ground was covered in large boulders and to one side, almost hidden from view a waterhole sparkling crystal clear in the sunshine.

"There," said Mchawi proudly, pointing his stick towards what looked like the entrance to a large cave. "The Elephant's Graveyard."

"That's why it is called a Sacred Mountain," whispered Becky in James ear.

As they walked closer it became obvious just how big the cave must be and guarding the entrance a troop of baboons who became increasingly aggressive and agitated the nearer they came and poor Ziwadi clung to Mchawi in fear. He stopped and raising his stick spoke in a commanding voice words James couldn't understand. The baboons became calm and there appeared on top of a huge boulder at the entrance to the cave, a pure white baboon. It was clear that he was their leader and one look from him subdued them all. Mchawi approached and sat down beside him.

"Lord Nyani," he said but the three friends could not understand the words he spoke. Ziwadi had now jumped onto Rory's shoulder for protection and she chattered excitedly watching Mchawi from a distance before he rose and beckoned the children forward.

"Come, come it is safe. Lord Nyani has allowed us to enter."

"I thought the idea of an Elephants Graveyard was just a legend, a myth," said James as they walked forward.

"So did we at first," replied Rory, "but now we know different."

Climbing over some boulders they entered an enormous cavern. 'I guess it needs to be large enough for elephants' thought James looking around at a space which made him feel very small indeed. As his eyes got used to the gloom, he could see the great cavern gradually sloped downward and Mchawi was beckoning them to follow.

"You must continue without me," he said, "I will remain here on guard as it would be dangerous for you all if any elephants came. Lord Nyani will warn me if any approach."

The cavern grew smaller as it descended downwards. In places the rocks glistened with water and became slippery, bats could be seen hanging from the ceiling. Although they had no torch to light their way the rocks seemed to emit enough strange light to keep the deep gloom at bay. Unexpectedly the cave opened up again into a cavern so large that the three friends could not see where it ended. From the ceiling high above hung gigantic stalactites and the floor was covered in the bleached bones and tusks of long dead elephants, it stood so high that it towered over the heads of Rory, Becky and James. They gasped in awe hardly able to believe their eyes or to comprehend the full magnitude of the scene in front of them.

"How on earth did they get here?" James whispered in amazement.

Rory and Becky shook their heads in disbelief as they had never witnessed this spectacle before.

"Mchawi will surely know the answer – let's go back and ask him."

Leaving the graveyard behind they slowly climbed back towards the entrance were Mchawi was sat waiting for them. They had so many questions but Mchawi held up his hand to silence them.

"You have been granted a very special privilege but we do not know all the answers nor are we meant too – not even the Mganga Nyeupe with his power can understand all the great mysteries of nature."

James stood open mouthed, still not sure if he believed what he had just seen. Had the magic of Rookery Manor travelled here to Kenya or was there magic everywhere? As though sensing his bewilderment the old man took his hand and looking deeply into James's eyes, he spoke again.

"In time you will understand many things – be patient and all will be revealed to you. Now young man you have seen the power of Mchawi but it must remain our secret, you must tell no one. Like your friends you have been given a great gift. You have been chosen to protect our wild creatures but much more than this is yet to be shown to you. Mtumwa would not bring you here if it were not so."

In silence, lost in their own thoughts they continued their journey back through the forest to the clearing were Mchawi lived, waiting for them beside the fire sat Mtumwa.

"Now my children you must let Mtumwa take you back home, for we will meet again soon, I am sure."

Bidding farewell to the old man, in no time at all they were all back at the waterhole and Kericho Plantation. James also had to say goodbye to his friends with a promise to see them again soon.

Lying awake that night, the events of the day were spinning around in his head. Mchawi had said that a different destiny awaited him and he had been sent to Kenya to fulfil something connected to Emily but what had she sent him there to learn and why? Would he find the answer among the other contents of the trunk? To James it seemed that the more he learned the more questions it created. Eventually sleep overcame him but as so often since his adventures began confused thoughts entered his dreams and seemingly unconnected images troubled his sleep.

Chapter 7 –
Adam Visits Rookery Manor

The half term holiday was almost at an end and James hadn't seen Adam for some time but the excitement of his last visit to Kenya and the Sacred Mountain would have to remain *his* secret for now though. His father was in London on business and would return to Rookery Manor in the evening, while his mother always went shopping on Friday mornings. Perhaps he could meet up with Adam and on the pretext of feeling lonely she might let him bring Adam around to the house. He had already told her on a previous occasion about his new friend in the village so it wouldn't be a complete surprise. Thankfully Adele Devonshire was far too preoccupied with Mrs Perkins and her shopping lists to pay too much attention to James's request waving him away with an impatient, "Yes, yes of course dear, now run along and play. I'll be back around 1 o'clock," she added for Mrs Perkins benefit and then hurried out of the house where Mr Perkins had her car waiting. Up until now James and Adam had always met in the woods but this was to be different.

"Mrs Perkins I want to invite Adam around; can you tell me where he lives?"

"Why, yes sure I can m'dear." And she went on to give him directions to the Petty's cottage on the edge of the village.

Taking a short cut across the fields it took him only about fifteen minutes to reach Bluebell Cottage. The white picket fence and gate looked in need of a coat of paint and the front garden, which had been a riot of summer flowers with yellow roses around the front door, now looked in need of attention. James tapped the knocker twice and heard footsteps hurrying towards the door which opened to reveal a lady not unlike Mrs Perkins. Wiping her hands on the flowery apron tied around her waist Mrs Petty spoke in the same country tones as the Perkins'.

"Well, young lad an' what can I do fer yeh?" she asked smiling at him broadly.

"I … I'm looking for Adam."

"Well, ain't you the lucky one, 'e's still 'ere – come on in then lad." And she opened the door wide inviting him to step inside. "An' what's your name then?"

"I'm James, a friend of Adam's."

"Oh, aye, he been tellin' us about yeh being the new folks up at the Manor 'ouse," she paused thoughtfully. "Didn't think you and our Adam would 'ave much in common though." With that she walked down the hallway and into the kitchen were Adam sat eating some toast and jam. At the sight of James, Adam's jaw dropped, his eyes opened wide in amazement and exclaimed, "What yeh doin' 'ere?"

"Manners Adam," his mother scolded, "yeh be polite when friends come a callin'."

"Sorry," said Adam almost choking on a piece of toast, "didn't mean to be rude."

"I just thought we could spend some time together before the school holidays finish," said James.

"There now, ain't that nice Adam," said Mrs Petty smiling at the two boys. "It's about time yeh had some friends from 'round 'ere," she added, busying herself once more at the kitchen sink.

Out of the window James could see the back garden of Bluebell Cottage planted with vegetables and beyond across the fields lay Rookery Wood. Adam fetched his coat and a scarf because although it was a fine day there was the chill of autumn in the air.

"Now, mind yer not late," his mother called after them secretly pleased that her son now had a friend of the same age. They might be posh folk she thought but yon lad seemed nice enough – polite too.

The two boys hurried across the field, kicking stones to see who could kick the farthest and laughing at nothing in particular. They paused to catch their breath watching it spread like a fine mist from their open mouths.

"Your mother's very like Mrs Perkins, our housekeeper," said James.

"O' course she is, they're sisters," replied Adam as though everyone knew that.

The boys chatted about this and that, things they had done since walking down Frosty Hollow when Adam had shown James the cave. Approaching Rookery Manor, James invited Adam inside but *he* was not at all sure 'them being posh and all' until James assured him it was OK with his mother, who wouldn't be there anyway. A few minutes later they opened the kitchen door and went inside, the warmth of the room embracing them after the chill wind outside. No sooner had they removed their coats than Mrs Perkins bustled into the kitchen.

"Good Lord, yeh gave me a proper fright," she exclaimed and then noticing Adam, "why Adam lad, nice to see yeh and the Young Master 'ere getting' on so well."

"Hello Aunty Poll," said Adam shyly, explaining how James had come to his house and invited him.

"'Ow about some of me scones and jam wiv a mug of 'ot milk to warm yeh up," she said to which the boys nodded licking their lips and beaming in anticipation. Once their appetite was satisfied, Mrs Perkins shoo'd them out of the kitchen and James led Adam upstairs to the attic. The door creaked less stiffly due to the number of times James had opened it since that first occasion. Switching on the light he led the way up the stairs.

"Gosh," said Adam on seeing the rocking horse then added. "Can I ride it?"

"Of course," replied James, "but close your eyes and let me know what happens."

Closing his eyes Adam began to rock back and forth. As if by magic he felt himself riding what seemed like a real horse of flesh and blood across the fields with the wind in his hair. "Giddy up, giddy up," he called as though urging the horse to jump the hedges that separated the fields. James knew how real it would feel to his new friend realising he had become so involved with the Cedar Tree, with Rory and Becky that he had forgotten the pleasure of riding Prince.

"Wow," exclaimed Adam opening his eyes, "that felt *so ... oo* real!"

"I know," said James smiling at the memory, "but I don't really know how it happens or why. But look here I've got something else to show you."

Taking the ribbon from around Prince's neck, James opened the trunk with the key and one by one he removed its contents.

"Where did they come from and what they doin' up 'ere?" asked Adam curiosity in his voice.

James realised in order to give him an explanation he would need to tell Adam all about Rory, Becky, Mtumwa and the Cedar Tree. Picking up the red silk scarf he opened it to reveal the diary and began the story of how he discovered its secret, travelling through time to find Rory and Becky. At first Adam didn't believe him saying it was just a story he'd made up but when James asked him to explain riding Prince he stopped and thought – that had seemed real enough! James stopped short of telling him about the Sacred Mountain, Mganga Nyeupe and the Elephants Graveyard. For now, that must remain his secret, after all he had sworn an oath to Mchawi that he would not reveal these things to anyone.

"I think they must have belonged to Emily and she left them here for someone to find. The rocking horse must have been hers too because it protects the key to the trunk," said James, adding, "Rory and Becky told me that grown-ups can't see either Prince or the trunk, to them the attic appears empty."

"Gosh," uttered Adam not sure what to make of it all. They examined each item in turn and when they came to the locket of golden hair Adam fell silent for a few moments, then in a hushed voice he said, "Yeh mean that this is a piece of 'er 'air … fer real – Emily what I seen at the cave?" and he looked at it with wonder in his eyes hardly able to comprehend that he held in his hand a piece of her that had survived for over 300 years.

"I think most of these things *must* have belonged to Emily," replied James breaking the silence and opening the book of pressed flowers to show Adam, who carefully read the notes she had made and finally at the end her name. As though in a trance Adam traced her name with his forefinger feeling an emotion he couldn't explain. James looked at him closely, sensing something but Adam said nothing. Curious to see what would happen, James handed him the strange piece of rock. Adam turned it over in his hand, peering closely at the metallic looking stone, watching how it glistened when the light touched it but he didn't cry out as James had when it became white hot. In fact, Adam's reaction was the same as Mr Wakefield's. Wanting to be sure, James asked him if it felt cold or hot to which Adam replied, "Naw – where did it come from?"

For now, James decided to pretend he didn't know and quickly put it back inside the trunk. Gathering up the other items he began placing them back but Adam seemed reluctant to let go of Emily's locket and pressed flower book. With a sad sigh he eventually allowed James to take them from his hand. Locking the trunk he put the key back around Prince's neck, suggesting they visit the guest room where Emily's picture had appeared. Closing the door to the attic they walked together down the corridor and James opened the door to the guest room. Adam followed him inside not sure what to expect.

"Did you feel cold when you came in?"

"A bit, why?"

"Because I've always felt something strange from the first time I came into this room. Then when the picture appeared and disappeared, I knew there had to be a reason. Rory and

Becky had discovered it used to be Emily's room and this is the only place in the house where she appears." They stared at the wall but nothing happened much to Adam's disappointment.

"She's only appeared to me once and I began to think I'd dreamt it but Rory and Becky said she only appears when something important is about to happen. I do sometimes feel her presence in the house though."

Adam looked thoughtful, slowly nodding his head in agreement although the only part he was sure of were the events he had seen in the woods and of course riding Prince, that had seemed real enough. The thing that connected them was the girl Emily so there must be something in it. Adam knew he wasn't the cleverest pea in the pod but even he realised there had to be a connection – the one puzzle was working out what and why?

"Come on," said James, "let's climb the Cedar Tree."

He wondered if Adam could also travel through time with him but it would not be today. They would just climb the tree like boys do and James showed him where he sat and Mtumwa appeared. It was obvious Adam was used to climbing as he was up in the tree before James took breath, sitting along the branch with his legs dangling down on either side while James sat in the hollow.

"Gosh, yeh can see fer miles and miles from up 'ere," said Adam straining his neck to see further. "There's Aunty Poll and Uncle Bert's 'ouse and me old school." His voice took on a sad note, Adam wasn't a great lover of school but now he had moved to the Comprehensive in town he liked it even less.

"Can't wait t' leave an' work wiv Pa on the farm," he told James, who wasn't brilliantly academic himself but generally enjoyed school although he had no particular idea what he would do when he left.

"Don't know 'ow yeh can stay there all week. Comin' 'ome is the best bit." That made the boys laugh.

"Come on, let's play football," James suggested, starting to climb down. They spent the next half hour releasing all their energy by kicking a football around beneath the Cedar Tree until Mr Perkins called to them it was lunch time and Adam's mother expected him home. Realising what a good time they'd had together their friendship was cemented from that point on although Adam suddenly felt a little shy, not sure what to say but James slapped him on the back with a grin and a promise to meet up again soon.

Chapter 8 –
The Hidden Grave

The weekend passed quickly preparing for school and Monday morning dawned wet and windy, a miserable day that echoed the mood enveloping James, he would not see Adam, Rory or Becky for at least another week. After Adam's visit, it had occurred to James that an investigation of the history around Rookery Manor and the village of Stanton Seymour during the time Emily had lived there might reveal something interesting. Possibly Mr Fothergill, his history teacher, might be able to help, he would surely know where James should look for such information.

Arriving just in time to put his belongings into the dormitory before the first lesson he was greeted by a couple of classmates and together they hurried downstairs to the Assembly Hall before class began. It was not until Wednesday morning though that he had the opportunity to talk with Mr Fothergill following a history lesson on the Tudors. James hung back while his classmates filed out to prepare for games.

"Please, sir, may I ask you for advice on a history matter?" Mr Fothergill smiled at James, 'at last a student genuinely interested in history' he thought.

"So, what can I do for you James?" he asked.

"Well, I was wondering where I could look for the history of my house and village in the eighteenth century?"

"My now, there's a thought." Mr Fothergill paused. "Does your village have a church?" he enquired.

"Yes, sir, but I've never been there."

"No matter. It's a good place to start particularly if it's old and existed during the time you are looking for. Old churches often keep records of village life and even old gravestones can be interesting. Of course, you could go to a local library if there is one and not to forget the internet. Type in your village, the dates you want and see what comes up. Let me know how you get on," he added.

James thanked him and quickly followed his classmates to games, mentally deciding to begin his search the very next weekend. He wondered if Adam would help him, after all two heads were better than one. First thing Saturday morning he would go and see him, maybe even exploring some of the local superstitions might point the way. Once the decision was made James wished the week would hurry by, he was eager to start his search feeling confident something important would be revealed.

Why is it, he thought, that when you want time to go fast it never does as the week seemed to drag and he found it increasingly hard to concentrate on lessons.

His mind would drift off to thoughts of Emily, imagining what her life might have been like and more than once he was brought up sharp by a teachers' strident tones telling him to pay attention and threatening detention – or worse! Strangely he also had a desire to explore the cave further but to do that he must persuade Adam to take him back there and to explore with him, even though he had seemed very reluctant before to go any further inside. Perhaps Adam was not as brave and adventurous as he tried to make out.

At last, the week came to an end and he was on his way home. Saturday was a cold morning but at least it was dry as James made his way to the Petty's house on the edge of the village. They had spoken on the telephone the night before so Adam was ready and waiting when James knocked on the door. Wrapped up against the cold they walked through the village towards the church, which being a Saturday morning was deserted. The church was very old, having been built centuries before even Emily had lived at Rookery Manor. Before beginning their search of the graveyard, the two boys couldn't help being curious to see inside. The big heavily carved door creaked as they pushed it open but no one was there. It felt cold with a damp, musty smell and ancient flagstones covered the floor with a number of uncomfortable looking wooden pews on either side. Weak sunlight was trying to lighten the stained-glass windows running the length of one side but it still appeared gloomy.

"Glad *I* don't 'ave to come 'ere on Sundays," said Adam.

"Me too," replied James looking around and noticing two alcoves on the opposite wall. Within each one was a plaque that appeared to be made of marble. They were carved and quite ornate with written text in the central panel. It was the second, older looking one that caught James's attention.

"Hey, Adam, look at this, it's got the Beauregard name on it – that must be Emily's father. Let's see what it says." James began to read the inscription out aloud.

"In honour of Charles Edgar Beauregard, resident of Rookery Manor in this parish. Benefactor to the Church of St Saviors in the village of Stanton Seymour in the year of our

Lord 1710. May the light of our Lord forever shine on Thee. For the blood of our Saviour sets all men free. In the sure, certain hope and strength of his power. To sustain your spirit in the final hour."

Adam looked puzzled. "What's that about then? What does it mean about bein' a Benefactor?"

"It usually means the person has given money, perhaps to save the church in some way. They obviously thought highly about Emily's father to put up this plaque to honour him. Let's look at the gravestones, there must be one for Emily and her father maybe that will tell us some more."

"OK," said Adam wrapping his scarf more tightly against the cold.

Not sure which was the oldest part of the graveyard the boys decided to explore a section each. Some headstones were so old and covered in lichen that it was almost impossible to read the inscriptions. There were others that looked like huge stone boxes sitting on top of the ground most of which seemed to be very old indeed and contained as many as three or four generations of the same family.

"Adam – quick come over here." James's excited voice carried across the graveyard in the still cold air. He was pointing to a neglected, overgrown area that looked as if no one had disturbed it for years. Most of the graves were surrounded by neatly cut grass and some contained flowers carefully tended by relatives and loved ones of the deceased but this part appeared to be forgotten and unloved, tucked away in a corner no longer used. 'It must be a very old part of the graveyard' thought James as he pulled away some of the vegetation that had almost hidden it from view.

"I almost missed it," he said as Adam joined him. "It was just something shiny that caught my eye."

"What was it?"

"Oh, only an old glass bottle but when I bent to pick it up, I realised there was an old gravestone behind all these weeds and look at the name!"

Adam peered at the section of grey stone that James had cleared and could just make out the name 'Beauregard'. He began pulling away some of the ivy which had grown over the headstone.

"It's full of dirt, let's try and clean it up a bit." James took a handful of twiggy leaves and began rubbing them over the headstone. Slowly the words engraved into the stone began to appear but it wasn't the name they expected.

"Here lies Constance Francine Beauregard 1682–1704 beloved wife of Charles and mother to a daughter Emily."

"Taken too soon. May she rest in peace."

"That must be Emily's mother but look at the dates, she died very young, only twenty-two. I reckon she died when Emily was born," James deduced. All this calculation was a bit beyond Adam but he nodded in agreement.

"Women often use to die having babies in those days. I remember our history teacher, Mr Fothergill telling us once." James didn't want to sound like a know-it-all.

"Look, there's more writin' further down." Adam was rubbing the stone with a piece of cloth he had taken from his pocket.

"If we had some water we could clean it better," said James looking around.

"I seen a tap where I was lookin' before – folks use it fer flowers." With that Adam marched off and returned a few minutes later carrying a flower vase full of water.

"I'll return it to the grave and put flowers back when we're finished." That explained were Adam had found it. The boys scrubbed at the stone as best they could and soon had uncovered enough of the engraved words to read:

Charles Edgar Beauregard 1678–1717

Emily Francine Beauregard 1704–1716

Nothing else, no words to say whether they were both buried there, no explanations of any kind.

"I think we should come back again and clean this up properly and remove the weeds," said James to which Adam agreed. "Maybe the vicar can tell us something."

"I think he's only 'ere on Sundays to take the service."

"Then we must come back tomorrow," said James realising that would mean he could not see Rory and Becky for at least another week but maybe he would have plenty to tell them by then. He also wanted Adam to show him the cave once again so they agreed to meet up that afternoon.

Chapter 9 –
The Glass Lake

Adam was already waiting for him beside the gate that led from Rookery Manor into the woods.

"What yeh doin' wiv a torch?" enquired Adam.

"I brought it so we could explore further inside the cave."

"Oooh, I dunno about that," replied Adam nervously.

"We've got to Adam. Look, we know that part of the woods is connected to Emily don't we, so maybe we might find some clues inside."

Adam had to agree it was possible and he could see James was determined – after all there was two of them, what could possibly happen. The boys chatted about their discovery at the graveyard that morning and in no time at all they were walking down Frosty Hollow. James had meant to memorise the way but they had chatted so much he knew he would never find it without Adam's help. As they approached the cave entrance James switched on the torch. Once inside they could see more clearly that although it narrowed at the end a passageway existed beyond.

James led the way with Adam holding tightly to his coat, he wasn't about to get lost in the dark. Bending down to avoid the roof of the cave they crawled along for about five minutes, scuffing their shoes on the uneven rock, then the passage opened wider and they could stand up once again. It reminded James of the Sacred Mountain and the Elephants Graveyard but there was no strange light from these rocks to illuminate their way. Adam had begun to feel a bit claustrophobic but he wasn't going to let James think he was chicken. Now that the passage had opened up he felt better but couldn't help wondering whether they might get lost and not find their way back.

Adam tugged at James's coat. "What if we can't find our way back?"

"There's only one passage so far," replied James hoping he sounded more confident than he felt. "We only have to follow it back and we'll be OK."

After a few minutes the passage opened out and eventually the two boys found themselves in another cave, much larger than the entrance. A shaft of light from high above pierced the gloom and shone onto what looked like a lake of glass. At some time, the rocks forming the roof of the cave had cracked and partially fallen in allowing light to filter through the vegetation growing in the woods above.

"What do yeh make o' this?" Adam's voice broke the silence. James bent down and his hand touched cold, clear water.

"Well, it isn't glass," he replied peering down into the water. There appeared to be shiny objects beneath the surface reflecting the light and giving the glass like appearance, although the centre of the lake looked dark, deep and forbidding. Stretching his hand down into the water James pulled out a piece of glistening metallic rock just like the one in Emily's trunk. He placed it on the floor of the cave were Adam immediately recognised it too.

"It's just like the one in Emily's trunk – do yeh think she found it 'ere?"

James wasn't sure, it seemed possible but how would Emily have found this cave? Just then Adam noticed another passage to one side of the lake. A sense of curiosity and excitement filled the two boys and all fear seemed to disappear.

"Come on James, let's find out where it goes."

Neither boy could explain why their fear had been replaced with a mounting sense of excitement. James dropped the piece of rock back into the lake and followed Adam, who had taken the torch and now led the way. Staying close together they followed the passage as it twisted and turned until finally, they came to a dead end.

Mystified Adam shone the torch all around, from side to side and up and down, then they realised there were steps hewn into the rock. Slowly and carefully so as not to slip, they climbed upwards. A trap door appeared above and at first attempt it wouldn't move.

"On the count of three let's push together." It creaked and James thought it moved. "Come on, let's do it again." Once more it creaked, the sound echoing eerily in the dark passage.

"I guess no one has moved it for years."

"Maybe it's locked – or overgrown wiv weeds," said Adam wondering where it had actually led them. Could they still be in the woods or had it led them to somewhere else. Walking in the dark had made it difficult to judge what direction they were walking in or how far they had come.

"We've got to give it another go," said James, "we've come this far we can't just leave without finding out what's on the other side."

Adam nodded and together they pushed with all their strength. Without warning something gave way and the door flew open with a loud bang as it clattered onto a stone floor above. The boys held their breath, not daring to move in case the noise had alerted someone – nothing, no loud voices asking, "Who's there?" Cautiously James peered over the edge and shone the torch into what looked like a cellar. Empty now, though it must have been used to store wine bottles at some time, a damp musty smell hung in the air, just like the church that morning, James shone the torch all around.

"Lord, look at them cobwebs." Adam whispered as he climbed into the room.

"Ain't nobody been 'ere fer yonks – wonder were 'tis?"

"Let's find out," said James noticing a light bulb in the middle of the vaulted ceiling. "There must be a light switch somewhere."

"There," said Adam pointing to the far side as James's torch lit up the wall and another door.

"What if this is someone's 'ouse, they might think we're burglars."

"It must belong to someone," James replied in a whisper, "we'll just open that door a tiny bit, carefully so as not to let anyone hear."

Putting his ear to the door Adam listened for any sounds coming from the other side but all was silent. Slowly he turned the door knob, as he did distant voices came from somewhere on the other side. Adam signalled to remain quiet and move back into the room, switching off the light which plunged them into darkness. Once by the trap door James could contain his curiosity no longer and whispered, "What did you hear?"

"Not what," said Adam, "but who. I couldn't 'ere what they was sayin' but I'd know them voices anywhere – 'twas my Aunty Poll and Uncle Bert."

"You mean our Mr and Mrs Perkins?"

"Yup. Like I said I'd know them voices anywhere."

"But does that mean we're in their house?"

"Naw, can't be, t'ain't near to Rookery Woods. Anyway 'tis to small fer havin' a cellar."

The boys looked at one another as the truth dawned on them but James voiced their thoughts first.

"Then it must be Rookery Manor," he whispered pausing to let the thought sink in before continuing. "I suppose it makes sense and answers the question about how Emily appears in the woods – she must use this passageway, or rather her spirit does."

Adam looked thoughtful. "But, were does that door lead to in yer 'ouse? Did yeh know about this cellar?"

"No," replied James somewhat mystified, "no one has ever said anything about a cellar underneath the house, not even Mr Perkins and he seems to know about all sorts of things."

"Look," said Adam, "no one's come through that door and it's all quiet now, let's try again."

Treading quietly the boys returned to the door and once again Adam tried the door knob. It turned quite easily but the door itself was stiff with lack of use and as the boys pushed together it scraped across the floor. Once more they held their breath in case the noise alerted someone but all remained quiet. When the door opened far enough for the boys to peer around, they saw a short flight of stairs with yet another door at the top. They glanced at each other questioningly. James shrugged his shoulders, shaking his head in mystified silence. Not wanting to make any more noise they both squeezed through the gap and began to climb the stairs pausing at the top to listen for any sounds – all was silent. Adam looked at James who nodded and grasping the handle he pushed the door but it didn't move.

"If no one knows about this place maybe tis locked and covered up," whispered Adam.

The disappointment and thought of re-tracing their steps back to the woods showed on their faces and their sense of excitement evaporated like a burst balloon. It had all been going so well, they had overcome every obstacle and to be defeated at the last moment by a door was too much. James stared as if willing it to open by magic and then he noticed the hinges were on their side.

"I think it might open towards us," he said to Adam, who grasped the handle pulling it towards him and almost falling backwards down the stairs as the door creaked open a few inches. They pulled together and it swung open to reveal the back of a large cupboard and shelves stacked with jars and tins of food – they were looking into the pantry of Rookery Manor.

"Well, I never," said Adam staring in disbelief.

"If we move these dishes on top of the shelf, I reckon we can just squeeze through if we're careful," suggested James, "then we can go through into the kitchen as Mr and Mrs Perkins should have gone home now." he added.

James went first, it was a tight squeeze and impossible not to make a mess. Adam followed.

"That's why no one knows about the cellar," James said leaning back over the cupboard to pull the door shut. "It looks exactly like the walls of the pantry from this side and I guess this old cupboard is so heavy it's not been moved for years."

The boys did their best to brush off the bits of dirt and replace the dishes to cover up any marks. Quietly they peered into the kitchen breathing a sigh of relief to find it empty. Just as they were about to congratulate themselves, James's mother burst into the kitchen with a large bag of potatoes which she almost dropped on seeing the boys.

"Good Lord, where on earth did you two come from – you gave me quite a fright." Then she noticed their dishevelled appearance. "Well, I don't know, you both look like you've been dragged through a hedge backwards – where *have* you been?"

The two friends looked at each other sheepishly and in unison replied, "In the woods."

"And what were you doing in the woods – digging for gold?" Turning her attention to James she added, "James, you had better get cleaned up before your father sees you and Adam you had better get home too. I don't know what your mother's going to say," she tutted in disapproval but smiled to herself – wasn't that just like boys.

Chapter 10 –
Raiders of the Sacred Mountain

James woke early next morning eager to meet up with Adam and continue their search for clues. The house was quiet as his parents never stirred before 9 o'clock on Sundays and the Perkins had the day off. He dressed quickly but before going downstairs for some breakfast he paused by the room next to his. A feeling of impending disaster came over him and he felt compelled to enter what he now called 'the cold room'. Even though the house was warm and he was fully clothed, James shivered as he stepped inside. Instinctively he knew that Emily's picture would be there as he turned to look at the wall. At first the picture frame was blank then slowly as though coming through a mist, Emily's face appeared.

This time she was not smiling, her expression looked troubled as she beckoned James forward. Gradually her face disappeared and he found himself staring at the unmistakeable image of the Sacred Mountain. As he watched, men appeared with guns and from behind the boulders a wave of angry baboons charged, led by the white albino, Lord Nyani. Shots were fired and Lord Nyani fell, his white fur stained red with blood. Many others also fell, no match for men with guns. The remainder fled in fear, their leader apparently dead, they scattered in panic.

James choked with rage as he realised their intention was to rob the Elephant Graveyard for the ivory. Tears ran down his cheeks at the heartless killing of Lord Nyani and so many innocent creatures. How had these men discovered the mountain's secret. The baboons had always kept people well away and only Mchawi was permitted inside. James rubbed the tears from his eyes and slowly the picture changed, it was Emily's face once more. Her expression and outstretched hands appear to be pleading with him but what could *he* do? Something shiny in her hand caught his eye, then he realised Emily was holding the piece of rock from the trunk, like those he and Adam had discovered the day before in the Glass Lake. It was as if she was asking him to take it. Then the truth dawned on him, Emily meant him to take the rock and somehow use it to save the Elephants Graveyard. As soon as James understood, Emily smiled and the picture disappeared.

Now what to do, he was supposed to be meeting Adam and so far, James had not told him about the Sacred Mountain. Turning the situation over and over in his mind, eventually reasoning that the more help he had the better chance of success, James decided the time had come for Adam to be told.

Slipping quietly up to the attic James wrapped the piece of rock in a cloth, putting it in his coat pocket along with the diary. Opening the door to his parents' bedroom he crossed to kiss his mother gently on the cheek. She stirred and opened her eyes in surprise. James whispered in her ear, "I'm going to play with Adam, don't worry I'll be back for lunch." His mother nodded and smiled; it was nice that James had made a new friend. She had been worried that he would feel lonely when they had moved out of London.

It was still early when James knocked on the Petty's front door. Adam hadn't even dressed and was eating his breakfast in the kitchen. James wasted no time in telling him what had happened that morning and suggested Adam should come with him.

"But 'ow do I tell Ma and Pa I'm going' to be away fer a long time?"

"No need," replied James. "The magic makes time different in the past. When I think that hours have passed with Rory and Becky in fact it's more like minutes when I get back home. Believe me your parents will never know."

"OK then, I'll get dressed and be with yeh in two shakes of a lamb's tail."

Before climbing the Cedar Tree, they checked that no one was around. All seemed quiet and in no time at all James was sitting in the hollow with Adam straddling the branch in front of him.

"Right," said James taking the diary from his pocket and beginning to read.

Adam felt a mixture of apprehension and excitement, he hardly heard the words James was reading before there was a sudden stiff breeze behind him and he felt a strange presence. James had stopped reading and whispered, "Mtumwa's here." Slowly Adam turned his head and found himself staring into the dark piercing eyes of a huge bird. His mouth dropped open, he couldn't speak and didn't know whether to be afraid or excited – James had told the truth after all! Signalling Adam to remain silent, James stretched out his hand towards the strange bird and instantly found himself in the Flame Tree but he was alone, there was no Adam. Disappointed but at the same time oddly relieved, he had not been sure how Rory and

Becky would have re-acted and maybe Mchawi would have been angry with him for revealing the secret to someone else. Assuming the magic didn't work for Adam, he climbed down to see his friends running towards him.

"James, James we are so glad to see you." Becky threw her arms around him with tears in her eyes.

"Has Emily appeared to you?" Rory's voice sounded serious. James nodded in response.

"I couldn't believe what she was showing me. They shot Lord Nyani and many of the other baboons but what can we do, surely it's too late?"

"Not necessarily too late." Rory assured him. "Remember Emily could see events before they happened so she sent you here because you had the means to help."

Remembering the rock in his pocket James removed it carefully as he wasn't sure whether it would turn hot again while he explained what had happened that morning. The three friends all stared at the strange piece of rock lying in James's hand glinting in the bright African sun. Wrapping it once again, he placed it back in his pocket.

"But how did *you* both know what was happening?"

"Mtumwa had disappeared for a few days but when he returned, he brought an urgent message from Mchawi who was summoning us all to the Sacred Mountain to prevent a terrible tragedy," Rory explained. "We felt pretty certain that Emily would appear to you."

"There's no time to lose," Becky's voiced urgently interrupted. "Now that James is here, we must meet with Mchawi straight away."

Nodding in agreement the three friends hurried to the stable yard and rode to the waterhole as before, were Mtumwa was already waiting for them. In no time at all they were in the forest clearing running towards Mchawi's hut. He was sat beside the fire with his head buried in his hands. On hearing the children's voices, he looked up and an expression of relief crossed his face. As always Ziwadi was close by and she began to jump up and down chattering excitedly.

"My children, you came." Machwi sounded relieved as he clasped their hands and turning to James said, "You have also been called from the future to help us avert this terrible tragedy."

"Yes," replied James, "but I really don't know why or how I can help."

"Surely the White Mganga is the only one with the power," Becky voiced all their thoughts.

Mchawi shook his head. "I don't know how the secret of the Sacred Mountain became known to these hunters. My powers seem to be fading." Shaking his head he paused and a troubled expression crossed his face. "What will become of the mountain, its people and the animals if I can no longer protect them?" his voice choked with emotion.

Becky tried to comfort him while Rory appeared embarrassed and unsure what to say. If this were true, life would change for all of them. Mchawi seemed to pull himself together and turning to James once more he asked him to relate the events which had brought him there. When James told him about the strange rock, Mchawi asked to see it. Taking it from his pocket, James carefully placed it in Mchawi's outstretched hands. Slowly it began to glow just as it had the first time James held it.

"It will become white hot and feel as if it's burning your hand," James warned him.

Mchawi smiled knowingly. "This rock has come from another world and contains powers greater than mine. It seemed to burn your hand James because you were not ready to receive its power. Come, hold it with me for I sense the time has come for you to learn your destiny."

James felt unsure and held back but Rory and Becky, both urged him to do as Mchawi asked. Placing his hands over those of the White Mganga, he could feel the warmth through the old man's hands and the rock glowed more strongly but this time it did not burn them. Slowly James could feel a strange heat creeping up his arms until it gradually filled his whole body. His heart began to beat faster but he was unable to draw his hands away.

"Do not be afraid, you will come to no harm. Let the power fill you as it is doing to me." Mchawi smiled and he no longer appeared to be a troubled old man but it was as if he had been reborn.

The rock ceased to glow and became cold. Mchawi handed it back to James.

"You now have the same powers as I do and together, we are strong enough to protect the Sacred Mountain. Trust me, the power will come to you when it is needed but we must waste no more time, I sense the hunters are getting close."

With that Mchawi picked up his stick. Ziwadi jumped onto his shoulder, chattering excitedly as she always did and the three friends followed them into the forest heading towards the Sacred Mountain.

Chapter 11 –
Rise of the Ghost Army

The forest was eerily quiet, not at all like the first time James had been there. It was as if the creatures of the forest knew that all was not well, even Mchawi sensed the change and quickened his step. They passed the deserted village with its ancient burial ground and began to climb the mountain slopes towards the Elephants Graveyard. I do hope we will be in time thought James anxiously. As if reading his thoughts Mchawi spoke aloud.

"If Emily can see the future, then she will have sent you in time James," he smiled reassuringly.

At that moment Becky let out a loud cry as she stumbled and fell to the ground. She had been walking a little way behind them but at the sound of her cry they all stopped and turned around. She sat awkwardly, holding her ankle, tears streaming down her face. Rory was the first to run towards his sister.

"What happened?" he asked anxiously as he tried to help her stand.

"My foot got caught in that hole and I think I've twisted my ankle," she cried trying to wipe the tears from her face.

"Can you walk?" asked James somewhat concerned.

"I don't think so," she replied, her voice trembling, the tears falling uncontrollably down her cheeks.

"Perhaps if you sit for a while," suggested James, "it might feel easier."

"I'll sit with her," said Rory suddenly becoming very protective. "But you and Mchawi *must* continue on. You are the only ones given the powers to save the graveyard. We promise to join you as soon as we can."

Reluctantly James had to agree and waved goodbye to his friends. Onward and upward they climbed until the forest gave way to the large clearing in front of the cave leading to the Elephants Graveyard. At first sight it appeared deserted. James's heart sank, were they too late and had Lord Nyani been shot had the baboons all fled. A troubled expression crossed Mchawi's face as he strode forward towards the cave entrance with James following closely behind. A sudden movement to one side startled him and then a feeling of relief as Lord Nyani appeared with several baboons cowering nervously behind him.

Mchawi stopped and suggested James remain while he went forward to speak with the white baboon, Guardian of the Cave. Even James could feel the tension in the air and all was definitely not as it had been the first time he had been brought there.

For many minutes the White Mganga and the white baboon sat on the ground in deep conversation before Mchawi rose to his feet and beckoned James. It appeared the hunters had already visited the cave but had not expected it to be guarded and the baboons had successfully driven them away. Lord Nyani however, knew it was only a matter of time before they would return armed with guns and prepared to shoot them all for the prize within the cave was too great to ignore.

"But how did the hunters find out about the cave?" asked James. "I thought the villagers regarded it as a sacred secret."

"They do," replied Mchawi, "but Lord Nyani thinks someone must have talked carelessly but he is not sure. Come James, we must enter the cave and prepare ourselves."

The baboons remained nervously on guard while James and Mchawi entered the cave and made their way to the Elephants Graveyard, still unsure of what to do. On reaching the huge cavernous graveyard Mchawi sat down and asked James to remove the strange rock from his pocket. As he did so a loud commotion and shouting echoed down from the entrance. They could hear human voices and the loud screaming of angry baboons. Quickly they made their way back to the entrance as shots rang out. Fearing the worst, they cautiously hid behind one of the large boulders and peered out into the clearing unable to believe the sight before them.

The hunters had indeed returned armed with guns and knives. Already many baboons lay dead and they feared for Lord Nyani, as Emily's vision had shown he also would be shot. A whimpering close by drew their attention, it was the white baboon and he was bleeding from his shoulder, thankfully he was not dead, only wounded. Then a familiar voice carried across the clearing – Rory's voice! James and Mchawi looked at each other puzzled, what was Rory doing with the hunters?

Slowly James peered out from behind their hiding place. Rory was indeed there but he was being held by two men and Becky was being carried by another it was clear they were not there by choice. Somehow, they had been captured by the white hunters and their African gunmen. Rory was struggling to get free and shouting loudly to warn James and Mchawi. Clearly the time had come to act if they were to save their friends and the Elephants Graveyard, but how? Then James remembered Emily's message telling him to take the strange rock from the trunk and then the words Mchawi had spoken. At that moment he knew what to do. Reaching into his pocket he took out the rock and handed it to Mchawi.

"No James, you also have the power, we will hold it together like we did before. Our joint powers will summon the Elephant Army, they will protect themselves."

"You mean a ghost army," whispered James.

Suddenly he understood everything. Their hands closed around the rock and immediately it began to glow.

"Picture the elephants as being alive, concentrate on nothing else, let it fill your mind and don't allow any other thoughts to enter."

Mchawi closed his eyes and James did the same. He could feel the power creeping through his body like a warm glow and he imagined all those bones coming to life. From somewhere deep inside the mountain came a rumble that grew louder with every second and the ground began to shake as though an earthquake was happening.

Mchawi smiled. "James, we have done it."

"You mean the ghost army."

"Yes, James they are coming, we are saved," he breathed a great sigh of relief.

It had taken very powerful magic indeed but down in the cavernous vaults of the Elephants Graveyard life had begun to stir. The spirits of long dead elephants began to rise from their slumber, like a white mist rising from their bones it began to take shape. At first it swayed back and forth as though gathering strength and purpose until finally the elephants ghost army appeared. A deep rumbling echoed through the cave and the ground began to tremble as though an earthquake had erupted from the bowels of the earth and the ghost army swept upwards towards the entrance of the cave.

From their hiding place behind the rocks James, Mchawi and Lord Nyani first felt a powerful wind, so strong it almost knocked them over. By now the hunters had also heard the frightening sounds echoing from deep within the cave and stopped in their tracks. In the commotion Rory broke free from the men holding him and ran towards Becky who had been dropped onto the ground.

"What's happening?" her voice trembled with fear, tears stained her sun kissed cheeks.

"I don't know," replied Rory holding his sister tightly. "I wonder where James and Mchawi are?" A sense of dread creeping over him like a cold sweat.

At that moment a loud trumpeting like a thousand elephants filled the clearing and from the cave swept a huge ghostly army.

The ground began to shake and tremble, the air was filled with screams and shouting. Some men tried to flee in fear but the white hunters stood their ground shouting, "It's not real, stay where you are." As they aimed their guns and fired into the midst of the ghostly army.

"You can't kill them; they are already dead," shouted one man as he tried to escape.

More shots rang out to no avail, the army just kept on growing as more and more elephants poured out of the cave until they almost filled the clearing leaving no escape for the hunters. A huge ghostly white bull elephant with magnificent tusks stood in front of the hunters and their men, panic etched on their faces but fear rooted them to the spot. Raising his trunk, a deep rumble echoed from the elephant's throat.

"You have violated the Sacred Mountain and sought what was not yours to feed your greed and for power. For this you will pay the ultimate price, I Methuselah have spoken."

As if to signal their agreement the whole ghostly army raised their trunks and trumpeted in unison – the sound was deafening.

All this time Rory and Becky had remained hidden on the edge of the clearing, afraid to move in case the ghost army should think they were with the white hunters.

"I hope Mchawi and James are safe somewhere," Becky voiced the thought in both their minds.

"So do I," whispered Rory, for even he could not be sure that Mchawi's magic was this powerful but if it wasn't Mchawi then who had brought this about? It never occurred to either of them that their friend James could be involved, after all the only magic he had possessed was that bestowed on him by Emily to travel back in time and visit them.

Still hidden behind the boulders at the cave entrance James too could not quite believe that he and Mchawi had created such amazingly powerful magic as the ghost army had swept passed them. From the safety of the rocks, they watched in stunned silence as Methusaleh spoke. James could not see either of his friends and hoped they were safe.

"I wonder what Adam would think of this had he been able to travel with me."

They could no longer see the white hunters and their men because they were completely surrounded by the ghost army and the sound of gunfire had stopped. Some of the hunter's men had dropped to the ground, grovelling in fear and pleading for their lives, for there was nowhere to run, no escape. Once more the old bull Methusaleh spoke.

"Never again will men come to the Sacred Mountain to steal what is ours and disturb our eternal sleep. What happens here today will be remembered forever and strike fear into the very hearts of men."

As though directed by some hidden signal the trumpeting began, building to a huge crescendo of ear-splitting sound, deafening the screams of the men who had come to rob the graveyard of its ivory.

For James and Mchawi the sound was almost unbearable as they crouched down behind the rocks and covered their ears. On the other side of the clearing Rory and Becky had moved deeper into the forest to escape the terrible sound which seemed to echo all around. Then as suddenly as it had begun the forest fell eerily silent. A wind came from no-where sweeping over the clearing and rushing into the cave entrance to disappear into the heart of the mountain. Mchawi peered cautiously from their hiding place and beckoned James to follow. Neither of them could believe the sight that greeted them, for the clearing was empty and still, no evidence of the hunters remained, it was as if their existence had been wiped off the face of the earth. Slowly baboons began to emerge from the forest and Lord Nyani appeared on his rock to signal that all was well.

Moments later Rory appeared supporting his sister hobbling on one leg, her ankle swollen from the fall. James rushed to his friends, relief on their faces they hugged one another with tears of joy running down their cheeks. Mchawi too was overcome with emotion and exhausted from the events they had just witnessed, he collapsed in a crumpled heap on the ground. A distinctive chattering from nearby alerted them to Ziwadi's presence, for she had disappeared, fleeing in fear with the baboons. Now she nuzzled Mchawi's ear, chattering excitedly as she usually did and their tears turned to laugher at her antics and the realisation that the danger had passed.

Life on the Sacred Mountain appeared to return to normal, danger had been averted. Rory and Becky were keen to know what magic had created the ghost army, so James related all the events to them. In turn they explained how the hunters had stumbled upon them as Becky had tried once more to walk with Rory's help. Until now Mchawi had remained silent allowing the children to talk but it was clear Becky would not be able to climb down the mountain without his help. Feeling rejuvenated since all his powers had been returned, Mchawi interrupted their conversation.

"I will use the strength of my new powers so you can walk again," he said.

Taking Becky's ankle between his hands, he began muttering strange words under his breath. She felt a warm sensation creeping into her ankle and it stopped throbbing with pain.

"Now you can stand," he said smiling, holding her hand for support.

"The pain has gone," she exclaimed in surprise, walking about and then jumping in the air just to prove it.

Mchawi interrupted them once more, "My children, you may remain here under Lord Nyani's protection but as Guardian of the Sacred Mountain I must visit the graveyard to see that all is as it should be."

"We're coming too," the three friends replied as one. They too wanted to see if the Elephants Graveyard had changed, so they followed Mchawi down the passageway that led to the cavern deep within the mountain. Everything looked exactly as it had before. Nothing seemed to have changed, not even a stalactite had been broken during the commotion as the ghost army had risen from the depths. Mchawi seemed pleased and a satisfied smile creased his old face.

"Aaah." He let out a deep sigh. "All has returned as it was before and our work here is done." He turned to James. "My child, you have today begun the long journey to fulfil your destiny and the great powers of the Universe who grant us the gift of magic will be pleased with you."

James felt both embarrassed by the words and at the same time curious as to what the old man meant. Becky's voice broke into his thoughts.

"What exactly happened Mchawi and how does this involve James?"

"Come, let us go back and I will explain all that I know."

When they returned to the clearing where Mchawi lived, he sat them down beside the fire and began to talk.

"The Great Spirit powers, somewhere out there." And he pointed to the sky. "Have chosen some of us for special deeds, some great, some small. I was chosen as the Guardian of the Sacred Mountain and given power to fulfil this duty. Rory and Becky's love of wild creatures and their desire to care and protect them has brought them to me. Before they came to

Africa, the girl Emily must have seen this in them for she too had been granted special powers. As for you James, I do not know your destiny only that you too have been given special power and there was a reason why you were brought to us today. Without your help we could not have roused the spirits of these sleeping giants that rest within the vast cave and the Elephants Graveyard would have been destroyed and with it the Sacred Mountain – life for many would have changed forever. It is to the girl Emily that you must look for the answers to your questions. Now children it is time for Mtumwa to take you all home."

Chapter 12 –
Adam Makes a Discovery

Lying in bed that night James was disappointed he had not had time to speak with Adam about the day's events because his parents of course thought they had been together that day playing in the woods.

On Monday morning he was back at school and James hoped Adam would understand and they could meet up the following weekend. He couldn't stop thinking about the event of Sunday and his part seemed like a dream. It was impossible that he, James Devonshire, should have been given the power to raise a ghost army from the bones of long dead elephants. It was a good thing his school friends knew nothing about his adventures as they would surely think he was mad and making up tall stories. Even Adam might find it hard to believe and he had seen Mtumwa. There were times when he had to pinch himself to believe it was real. All the adventures that had happened since he left London to live in Rookery Manor and if Mchawi was right, they had only just begun.

"I wonder if Adam has found out anything more about the Beauregard family?" he mused aloud to himself.

"Talking to yourself is the first sign of madness and who's Beauregard anyway?"

The voice behind made him jump, so deep in his thoughts James hadn't heard one of his classmates come up behind him.

"Gosh you startled me Richard, I didn't hear you."

Richard Andrews could be a bit of a nosey, busy body and not a particular friend of James, so he ignored the latter part of the question.

"Hey, Devonshire, I asked you a question. Who's Beauregard?" His tone insistent and more than a little threatening.

"No one special, just a relative." Hoping that would satisfy him and for the moment it seemed to as he walked off with a grumpy shrug of his shoulders. Thankfully his two school friends, Thomas and Patrick, arrived to tell him all their news, which in comparison to James's weekend was pretty tame.

The school week passed much as usual and soon it was Friday. Saying goodbye to his friends James hurried down the great staircase to the entrance hall where his father was waiting for him. On the drive home his father was always interested to hear about his week at school and how well he was doing. John Devonshire hoped one day James would become something 'big' in the city, why else would he be paying a small fortune for a private school. James on the other hand had no such grand plans and was more interested in discovering his destiny from Emily just as Mchawi had told him. He often wondered what his parent would think if they knew all the adventures that had happened to him since coming to live at Rookery Manor – no doubt they would accuse him of telling lies and making up stories, which would be understandable after all.

Saturday morning dawned bright but cold and James could hardly wait to meet up with Adam and find out what had happened when Mtumwa whisked him off to Kenya leaving Adam behind. He was unsure how much to tell Adam about the battle to save the Elephants Graveyard. It might be hard for his friend to believe and James had made a solemn promise to Mchawi in the beginning not to reveal its existence to anyone and he assumed that included people in the future as well.

The two friends agreed to meet up at the village church as Adam said when James telephoned him that he had more information about the Beauregard grave they had discovered together the week before. The wind was bitingly cold and James wrapped the scarf around his neck and tucked the ends into his coat as he hurried through the village. Adam was already waiting inside the church, at least it was a bit warmer there. Feeling a little self-conscious they were unsure whether to hug each other but, in the end, settled for "Hi." James was eager to know what Adam had discovered about the Beauregard grave but Adam got his question in first.

"I couldn't' believe it when yeh disappeared in front of me eyes and that darn big bird, I ain't never seen nothin' like that, ever. Where did yeh go?"

James then had to spend some time explaining what happens when he travels back in time to visit Rory and Becky. Adam had to admit at first, he had found it difficult to believe James until the big bird arrived and they both disappeared.

"I guess that bit of the magic doesn't work for you." James hoped he sounded disappointed for Adam.

"So, what happened after yer gone? Yeh know wiv the picture and what yeh said Emily told yeh and all that?"

During the past week James had changed his mind so many times before finally deciding that he would tell Adam part of the story but not the part that mentioned the Sacred Mountain and all that had taken place there. Adam might not have been clever but he had a good memory.

"When yeh told us last week about Emily's picture yeh said some tragedy were about to 'appen and yeh had to help."

James had thought about that too. "You know I told you Rory and Becky help the animals; well, they were trying to stop poachers killing some elephants for their ivory and three of us had a better chance of success than two."

Adam looked thoughtful as though he wasn't entirely sure of James's explanation but slowly nodded his head. James hoped the explanation would satisfy him for now and to prevent further questions he quickly asked Adam to tell him his news.

"What happened after I disappeared?"

"Well," Adam paused for greater effect. "I sits there fer a while, thinkin' yeh might come back soon and when yeh didn't I climbed back down and went to the church like we'd first planned."

When he arrived the Sunday service was taking place so he went first to the grave and attempted to clean it up a bit more. After the service finished and the people had all gone, he crept into the church before the vicar left.

"E remembered me from the village and when I asked 'im about the Beauregard grave we discovered and the plaque on wall, 'e took me down the steps at back of the church."

"What for?"

"T'show me some big 'eavy books all about the church and village fer 'undreds of years. Seems I made 'im curious about the grave so we looked in them books fer answers."

"Did he find any?"

"Well, sort of. 'E showed me this big book, it were very old and the writin' were difficult to read, so 'e read it to me."

"So, what did it say?" James was getting impatient and wanted to know what Adam had learnt.

"I'm gettin' to it," replied Adam, a little sharply.

"Sorry, go on."

"Well, them Beauregards were the richest people in these parts and he built your 'ouse."

"I already know that," said James sounding a bit cross …

"Yeah, but yeh didn't know that 'e also built the village church, well sort of re-built and made bigger, 'cos before it were just a small stone buildin'." Adam suddenly felt very important and knowledgeable. "When Emily's ma died, after havin' her, she was buried in the grave we found. It were meant to become a family …" Adam paused with a puzzled look on his face. "Vicar did tell me but I can't remember what he called it."

"A Mausoleum?" suggested James who had heard his father talk about such things when they lived in London.

"Yeah, that sounds a bit like it. Anyhow, he didn't start to build it 'til Emily had grown a bit and it still weren't finished when them village folk killed 'er 'cos they thought she was a witch. They buried her wiv 'er Ma but when Pa Beauregard got killed some men from the village took axes n' things an tore down the … what you said. They wanted to destroy the grave as well but the vicar what lived then stopped 'em. Told 'em they'd burn in hell forever and ever if they touched a sacred burial place. That's why there's nowt on the grave but names and dates. Over the years it got forgotten 'til we found it." Adam finished with a note of triumph.

"Did the book say all that? How incredible!"

"Not really but vicar said from what were written that was what must 'ave 'appened. The books were written wiv important things that 'appened in the village."

"Great work Adam but I'm not sure whether this information has given us anymore clues. I think we'll have to put down the things we know and see what we find."

Adam looked thoughtful. "Why don't we look at 'er book again 'cos we 'aven't looked at it all."

James had to agree and suggested Adam call at the house in the afternoon. The boys went their separate ways and James promised to look more closely at Emily's diary. Knowing his mother and father were going to Bath shopping after lunch they would be undisturbed for a few hours.

Chapter 13 –
Emily's Diary Reveals a Secret

With lunch cleared away his mother busied herself preparing to go out, scolding James to hurry up and get himself ready.

"I'm spending the afternoon with Adam."

"But you've already been together all morning," his mother said crossly.

"I know, but he has a project he wants me to help him with and I promised."

James hoped she wouldn't ask about the 'project' and just assume he would be at the Petty's house – he didn't *really* want to lie to her. Fortunately, his father came in at that moment and convinced his wife it would be fine, after all it wasn't as though they were going to leave him at home alone, he would be at the Petty's house. James breathed a sigh of relief as his mother gave him a key to the back door with strict instruction to lock up and go straight to Adam's house.

The moment his father's car drove out of the driveway and disappeared down the road James hurried up to the attic and took Emily's diary out of the trunk. At first sight it appeared as before just a book of pressed flowers with dates and locations but on closer inspection he realised that some pages had more writing than he'd noticed before. On one page, dated 10th March, she had written:

"I disobeyed Father today and explored the passage that goes out of the cellar. It was *very* dark and even with a lighted candle difficult not to slip down the steps. I came to a large cave and in the middle was a deep pool of water like a lake of glass. Just below the surface I could see a number of shiny objects so I reached down and took one in my hand. It was a strange rock, glinting like polished metal in the candle light. Something compelled me to put it in my pocket and later I placed it in my box of treasures. I didn't dare explore further in case the candle went out and I became lost."

So *that* is how it came to be in her possession thought James, but at that point she didn't realise the passage led to the woodland glade. Examining the pages one at a time he found more writing dated sometime later, which read:

"I have always known the birds and animals didn't fear me but something strange has happened since I found the shiny rock in the Glass Lake. When I held it in my hand, it glowed bright and I felt a warmth creeping over me but I didn't feel afraid. Now I find I can understand what the birds and animals are saying, sometimes they talk to me in the garden or when I walk in the woods."

At that moment it became clear to James that the strange rock had given magical powers to Emily all those centuries before in the same way it had happened to him and Mchawi. There was no time to read further as a loud knocking could be heard at the kitchen door. Hurrying downstairs, he knew Adam had arrived.

"Sorry Adam I didn't realise what the time was, I've been reading Emily's diary. Come on up to the attic and I'll show you," he said excitedly, making Adam extremely curious. Once in the attic James showed Adam the written pages.

"So that's 'ow she got 'er magic powers," he paused thoughtfully. "Do yeh think all them other stones in the lake give the same powers if yeh touch 'em?"

James shrugged his shoulders, "Dunno, they might." But he didn't voice the thought that came into his head and Mchawi's words that it only happened when the time was right. They continued to turn over more pages until they came to another entry dated weeks later. There were bright yellow primroses and celandines together with small green fern fronds pressed together into a bouquet, looking as fresh as the day they were picked. Beside it, Emily had written:

"I walked down Frosty Hollow today, so pretty in the spring, and sat for a while in the woodland glade with the deer. It was a lovely warm day but a sudden cold wind made me shiver and the deer ran into the wood as if they had been frightened. A strange feeling that something terrible was about to happen descended like a dark cloud. The glade disappeared and I saw the village, a cottage was on fire and people were running with buckets of water but it was hopeless, it burnt to the ground and with it a mother and child. I sat and cried with despair before running home to tell Father of the accident but he just laughed and said I had been dreaming – there had been no fire in the village. But it had seemed so real, how could that be, what had happened to me?"

The next pages were filled with drawings of the garden and more pressed flowers but then a few pages on she wrote:

"My heart is filled with sadness and my tears will not stop falling. Today a house in the village burnt down, nothing is left and poor Mr Farthingdale has lost his wife and tiny baby. I feel I will never write in my book again."

James and Adam looked at one another, an expression of shock and disbelief on their faces.

"She'd been given a vision before it 'appened," whispered Adam softly.

"And no one believed her," James replied, a note of sadness creeping into his voice.

For quite a while the two boys sat in silence, each lost in his own thoughts before they looked at the book again. It was some time before her book once more became filled with flowers and happy things. The afternoon was now getting late and it would soon be dark now winter was approaching. As the boys wondered what to do next the sound of a car was heard crunching up the gravel driveway – Mr and Mrs Devonshire were back.

Locking everything back into the trunk the boys hurried down the stairs just as Adele Devonshire opened the front door almost tripping over the step in her surprise.

"Goodness," she exclaimed, "I didn't expect you to be home," turning to Adam she said, "Well hello, you must be Adam I suppose," to which Adam simply nodded as though struck dumb. "Perhaps you would both help your father bring in the shopping." With that she swept down the hallway towards the kitchen.

After helping with the shopping Adam said he needed to be going home before it got too dark but maybe they could meet up again on Sunday. James waved goodbye as Adam hurried down the drive and turned towards the village. He would have liked to return to the attic and explore Emily's book some more but decided it would be better to spend some time with his parents as he had seen very little of them that day. There was no thought of seeing Rory and Becky, he needed to find out more from Emily's book as Mchawi seemed to think the clues to his destiny lay with her.

James woke early the following morning; the house was still quiet and the world outside seemed still and silent. As he peered out of the window and pulled back the curtains, he could see a light frost covered the lawn and a layer of thin ice lay over the pond. Autumn was coming to an end and the first signs of winter were approaching. He wondered what the winter would bring and hoped that Christmas would see the woods and fields covered in snow. He imagined Emily dressed in a white fur coat and hat, almost invisible against the snow, possibly feeding the birds with scraps from the kitchen. I don't suppose they had bird seeds in those days, he mused exploring this imaginary picture he had conjured up of what winter might have been like for her. Pulling on his dressing gown he ventured out onto the landing and opened the door to the 'cold room' hoping that Emily might appear to him but the wall remained blank. Disappointed James returned to his bed and pulled the covers tightly around him thinking about Emily's book and the words she had written. After what seemed like hours James heard his parents going downstairs and knew that breakfast would soon be ready.

Once breakfast was over James made an excuse that he had homework to finish in his room but what he really wanted was to read more of Emily's diary. Creeping quietly into the attic where his breath hung like a fine mist in the chill air, he retrieved her book from the trunk and took it back to his warm, cosy bedroom. Sprawled on his bed he turned the pages until he found the passage they had read the previous day. There were more pages filled with drawings and pressed flowers but in between James discovered other times when

Emily had visions of things that had not yet happened. At first people apparently just laughed at her and took no notice until they began to realise things were happening just as she had said. That was when people began to call her a witch, accusing her of bringing bad luck into the village. Her father forbade her to speak of such things ever again and never to go into the village alone. He feared for her safety knowing the rumours that were being voiced by many villagers, yet he felt unsure as to what to do for the best. In her final entry James could feel her despair.

"I do not know what will become of my life, Father only allows me outside in the garden. The birds and squirrels visit me and sometimes I sit in the shade of the Cedar Tree listening to the rooks squabbling above. I have found a secret passage that takes me into the woods where no one can see me, there I feel happy and free. The pretty Roe deer come and talk to me, then I forget my troubles for a while until I must return home, which now seemed like a prison."

Some of the words were smudged as if she had been crying as she wrote them down. James felt a lump in his throat as he realised it would not be long before she would be poisoned and die. It was almost as if she knew somehow because in the last page she simply wrote: "This book belongs to Emily Beauregard 1716."

James read and re-read her last entry, realising that at some time she must have explored the passage beyond the Glass Lake and discovered it came out in the woodland glade, that must surely be what she meant by 'a secret passage into the woods'. "I wonder what Adam will make of this when I tell him," he muttered.

At 11 o'clock prompt Adam knocked on the kitchen door and Adele Devonshire invited him inside before James could reach it.

"Hello again Adam," she smiled disarmingly. "James has been telling us all about you. (Which wasn't entirely true) Come on into the warm kitchen, you must be frozen, it's very cold out there." Before James could say a word, she continued, "And what are you two boys going to do today?"

Adam quickly replied, "I'm takin' James to see 'ow pretty the woods are when it's frosty."

"And we'll probably play football," added James quickly, anxious to escape before his mother started asking awkward questions, knowing Adam felt a little uncomfortable. "We'll be back in time for lunch," he called out as an afterthought.

Soon they were walking down Frosty Hollow, which did look very pretty with a light dusting of frost covering the branches and ferns. It had already begun to disappear from their lawn but here in the Hollow the sun's warm rays would take much longer to reach beneath the overhanging trees. James began to tell Adam what he had read and so engrossed were the boys they hardly noticed the cold. On reaching the glade they sat down on the rocks and James took Emily's book from his pocket showing Adam the last entry.

"So, you see at some point she must have explored beyond the Glass Lake and discovered it led here."

"She must 'ave been brave to explore all by 'erself," said Adam knowing how nervous he had felt and James had been with him for company.

"Yes, or desperate to find a way out," added James.

Adam nodded thoughtfully. "I wonder if she was ever sorry she'd discovered them magic rocks?"

The boys sat in silence for a few minutes lost in their own thoughts.

"Maybe if we come 'ere one night when the moon's full she might be sat 'ere and we could ask 'er."

James wasn't at all sure about coming to the woods at night, suppose his parents discovered he wasn't in the house, they'd have seven fits and ban him from going out, then he'd be like Emily. At that thought James shivered but not with the cold. It had also occurred to him that the glade, cave and Glass Lake might not be as far from Rookery Manor as they had first thought. After all, when they had explored the hidden passage, it hadn't taken them as long as it did when they walked through the woods and down Frosty Hollow. He was conscious of Mchawi's words about his destiny and couldn't help wondering how all this fitted in. Did Adam have a role to play and if so, what was it? Although Adam shared many things about Emily, he had not been able to travel back in time with James, so maybe the magic wasn't meant for him. The more James thought about everything the more confused he felt.

"Gosh Adam, I'm freezing let's go back to the house and play football."

"OK." After a short pause Adam added, "Do yeh ever wonder why she appears in the picture and why she left 'er book and them things in the attic … and why you can go back in time, an I can't?" a note of disappointment crept into his voice.

James had to admit he did wonder but so far had no answers. Reluctant to repeat Mchawi's words about his destiny he simply replied, "Rory and Becky seem to think Emily will tell me eventually, when the time is right."

In no time at all they were walking through the gate into Rookery Manor. Still feeling cold they decided to go inside first to warm themselves in front of the kitchen range. James mother was busy cooking and his father had gone to the village pub as had become his custom lately, something to do with getting to know the local's he had said!

Adam whispered in James's ear, "Do yeh think I could ride that rockin' horse again?"

James nodded and the boys disappeared upstairs, his mother too busy to notice what they were doing. Creeping up into the attic and closing the door behind them Adam sat astride Prince, stroking his mane as though he were a real horse. James took the key from around the horse's neck to return Emily's diary to the trunk but before he could do so Adam reached forward and took it from his hand.

"Give it 'ere a mo', I want to look at sommat'." Turning towards the end of the book Adam stopped and showed the page to James.

"See 'ere, we almost missed it 'cause we were lookin' at the flowers but between them flowers she's drawn a map. Look." Adam pointed to the page.

The writing was so small but between the pressed flowers was a map of Rookery Woods with Frosty Hollow and the woodland glade. Even the Glass Lake was marked with a line and the passage to the cellar of Rookery Manor. It showed quite clearly, they were actually much closer to the house than they had realised. The boys had actually walked to the glade and the cave in a very roundabout way. When Adam explored the woods, he came from the fields near to his home and not the path from Rookery Manor at all, so the boys had always gone the way Adam knew.

"Well, I never," exclaimed James, "that explains why we came up into our house so soon."

Adam had begun to rock slowly back and forth on the rocking horse as he read Emily's last words.

"I wish I could make her 'appy and free forever and she'd never eaten them poisonous mushrooms." Closing his eyes, he began to rock back and forth, faster and faster.

James shivered even though strangely it felt unusually warm in the attic despite the bitter cold outside. Suddenly Adam and Prince disappeared and he was left looking at an empty space beside the trunk, the key on its ribbon and Emily's diary lay on the floor.

Chapter 14 –
Adam's Journey to the Past

To Adam it seemed a terrible tragedy that Emily should be murdered just because the villagers were afraid of her and thought she was a witch. In his heart he wished there was a way he could protect this girl he had never know and yet felt such a close bond with. Like him she had loved the woods and wild creatures living there. He read and re-read her last words, imagining her delicate face and that golden hair he had touched in the gold locket, as he rocked back and forth, faster and faster. It was as if he was riding Prince through the woods, he could even hear the sound of many horses and people shouting. Through the trees a group of horsemen thundered past him as though he wasn't there. Adam thought it odd as they were dressed in strange clothes and had not appeared to see him or Prince. Then he realised that Prince was no longer a rocking horse instead he was actually sat astride a real live breathing white stallion as beautiful as any horse he had ever seen but he was no longer in the attic and there was no James with him.

He recognised Rookery Woods and somehow knew that the other horsemen must have been out hunting deer but nothing else made any sense – was it a dream?

How could he possibly fall asleep riding a rocking horse in James's attic or maybe that was part of the dream, he pinched himself hard.

"Ouch, that hurt," he exclaimed out loud.

Now this was getting scary, if it was a dream, he shouldn't have felt that. Panic rose from the pit of his stomach and almost choked him, what had happened and how?

"There's only one way to find out." Adam said to himself taking a deep breath to steady his nerves. "I've got to ride this 'orse and see if Rookery Manor is still there." Somewhat tentatively he shook the reins. "Come on giddy-up, Prince."

To his surprise the horse started trotting forward, slowly at first until Adam's confidence grew, it was as if the horse knew exactly where to go. They emerged from the woods and there was Rookery Manor, Adam breathed a sigh of relief and yet there was something different about it. They went through the gate and into the garden, the tall Cedar tree was there and the pond. Adam knew he hadn't taken much notice of James's garden but instinctively he felt it was not quite the same and what would James's parents think if they saw a horse riding across their lawn, he'd be in awful trouble and probably not be allowed to see James ever again. He could always blame the horse but how would he explain finding and riding it from the woods.

"There you are Prince wherever have you been. I thought I'd lost you or someone had stolen you."

Adam turned around as a young girl with fair golden hair and soft blue eyes ran toward them. Gently stroking the horse's neck, she kissed it lovingly on the muzzle. Taking hold of the reins she began to lead the horse towards the house but seemed completely unaware of Adam's presence as though he were invisible to her. Just then a man came out of the manor house and like the girl their clothes were like something from an old history book.

"Look, Father, Prince has come back he wasn't lost or stolen after all."

Slowly the truth began to dawn on Adam. Somehow, he had been transported back in time and was looking at Emily Beauregard and her father – but why couldn't they see him? Surely it didn't make sense if Prince had brought him here it must be because Emily had made him, so why couldn't he speak to her?

Frustrated Adam waved his hands in the air and shouted, "Hey, I'm Adam. I've come 'ere like yeh wanted – I've come to save yeh." But it made no difference the girl and her father continued to talk as though he didn't exist.

Emily and her father led Prince around the house to some stables while Adam sat on the horses back feeling afraid but unsure of what to do. Emily was obviously excited at Prince's return, clapping her hands in delight as her father led the horse into the stable, removing the reins while she gave Prince an apple.

"Now my darling daughter let us lock him safely in for the night and retire to the kitchen for supper."

The stable door closed and Adam was plunged into darkness. He could smell the hay and Prince's warm breath but the dark enveloped him like a cloud and once more he could feel panic rising from his stomach like a thousand butterflies. Blinking in the gloom he hoped for inspiration or at least to see his surroundings. Slowly at first a tiny point of light appeared ahead of him, gradually increasing in size until suddenly it exploded into a blinding flash. He thought he could hear a voice calling him from a distance.

"Adam, Adam, where did you go?"

It felt as if he was being woken up from a deep sleep and then he realised it was James's voice and he was back in the attic sat on Prince, the rocking horse.

"What happened Adam, you were rocking faster and faster and suddenly you and Prince disappeared, I couldn't believe it. I thought I was having a terrible dream then as suddenly as you disappeared you were both back again."

Slowly Adam got down from the rocking horse looking slightly stunned and relieved at the same time.

"Yer not goin' to believe what just 'appened to me, can't quite believe it meself." He sat on the attic floor beside James and began to describe the events he had just experienced.

"But what I don't understand is, if Emily's magic took me back to 'er time, why couldn't she see me? I mean what good is that?"

James felt as mystified as Adam. Somehow Adam's wish to 'free her forever' while reading the book and riding Prince had conjured up the magic that sent him back in time to Rookery Manor when Emily lived there but it didn't make sense if she couldn't see him. They must be missing something, but what? If he hadn't seen them disappear with his own two eyes, James would have thought Adam dreamt it but the fact was, something had caused Adam and Prince to vanish from the attic.

The bridge between past and present for him was the Cedar tree just as it had been for Rory and Becky. Now it seemed that Prince, the rocking horse, was also a means to transport someone from the present into the past but *whose* magic was responsible? Surely if it had been Emily Beauregard she would have wanted to talk to Adam and explain why, or, another thought came into James's mind. What if it had not meant to be Adam at all but him, that might explain why she couldn't see him but James decided to keep that thought to himself for now. It had become increasingly obvious that Adam was developing what James and his school friends would call a 'thing' for Emily and to crush his feelings at this point would be rather cruel, they really needed to find out the truth.

"You've gone all quiet, what yeh thinkin'?" Adam's voice broke into his thoughts.

"Just trying to make some sense of it all but I can't," replied James. "I was wondering whether Rory and Becky might know something from when they lived at Rookery Manor."

In actual fact James had really wondered if Mchawi had the answer but so far Adam knew nothing about him.

"When yeh come 'ome from school next weekend can yeh ask 'em," Adam pleaded, he was quite desperate to find the answers. James promised he would try and they could meet up again the following Sunday.

Chapter 15 –
A Compass and a Ball
of Silk Thread

The ruler hit his desk with a loud thwack and James nearly jumped out of his skin.

"I know maths is not your favourite subject Devonshire but if you are to stand any chance of passing your exams, you need to concentrate." Mr Porter the maths teacher's voice thundered around the classroom. Richard Andrews sniggered but Mr Porter rounded on him.

"You do that once more Andrews and it will be detention for you. Class, pay attention."

James knew he had allowed his thoughts to stray once more to the events of the past weekend and tried to concentrate on the blackboard but was conscious of Richard Andrews glaring menacingly at him and mouthing some silent threat. He really was a horrid boy and a bit of a bully, James generally kept out of his way. Apparently, he had a difficult home life with a very strict father who had little time for emotions and feelings. James assumed that was why he behaved that way at school and most boys tried to avoid him, if at all possible, which probably made him worse. James smiled and shrugged his shoulders hoping that would pacify him. The bell sounded for the end of morning lessons and thankfully Thomas and Patrick whisked him away to the Refectory before Richard could do anything.

"What's up James," said Patrick, "it's like you've been in another world all week."

"Yeah, like here but absent," laughed Thomas.

"Sorry chaps, I've just got things on my mind," replied James hoping they wouldn't ask too many questions.

"Nothing serious I hope." Patrick sounded concerned.

"No, no," said James thinking fast. "Just one of my old friends from London, his parents are splitting up." He was not one normally given to telling lies but he could hardly tell them the truth and expect to be believed.

"How awful for him but it happens." Thomas shrugged and changed the subject.

James was grateful for their friendship, it made school away from home more tolerable especially now that he had Rory, Becky and Adam with all the magical adventures they had together. The remainder of the week passed uneventfully and soon he was back home once again. For Adam's sake he knew he must keep his promise to visit Rory and Becky but it wasn't until after lunch he was free to climb the Cedar Tree. Wrapped up against the cold James wondered if the winter weather would make climbing the Cedar tree impossible?

The wind was bitingly cold on his cheeks so he never felt the whoosh of Mtumwa's wings as he alighted on the branch in front of him but soon the cold was replaced by the intense heat of the African sun and Becky's voice was calling him. Overjoyed at being together again the three friends sat on the grass beneath the Flame tree while James told them all about Adam's adventure and their discovery in the graveyard. They too were puzzled by Emily's apparent inability to see Adam even though she must surely have been the one to transport him there.

"I think there is only one person who might know the answer," voiced Rory.

"Exactly," said James. "I felt we had to ask Mchawi, which is why I'm here hoping you can take me to see him."

"Then let's hurry and ride to the waterhole," said Becky, "we haven't seen him ourselves since the raid on the Sacred Mountain and you discovered your magic powers. I'm sure he will be able to help."

Mchawi was indeed delighted to see them and reported that all was well on the Sacred Mountain now. Rumours about the disappearance of the white hunters had spread among the villages and superstitions created about great and powerful spirits living on the mountain, people were now afraid to venture beyond the lower wooded slopes.

"So, you see James together we did a great thing but I think you have need of my help in some way?" Mchawi inclined his head and looked questioningly at James.

They all sat down in front of Mchawi's hut and James began to tell him about Adam's adventure and the questions they could find no answers for. James had hoped Emily would appear in the picture and explain everything to him but that hadn't happened.

"You had the power to conjure Emily's face in the fire the first time I came, so I am hoping you can find the answers," said James.

"I will try my child, for it is thanks to you that my powers have been restored even more strongly."

Mchawi disappeared into the hut and returned with the large bowl which he placed on the fire. Taking a handful of magic dust, he threw it into the bowl where it burst into flames and Mchawi began chanting in a strange voice as he danced around the fire, the necklace of bones and shells banging together with a hollow sound. The white mist began to rise from the bowl and circle the White Mganga until, like the first time, it settled above him like a huge white cloud.

The children waited hardly daring to breathe in case they broke the spell, watching the cloud to see what would be revealed. Emily's face did not appear this time but out of the mist James recognised the attic at Rookery Manor. He heard Becky gasp in recognition as her voice whispered, "The attic." The image became blurred and when it cleared there was Emily's trunk of special treasures. The lid was open and as they watched, items inside flew out and landed on the floor. The gold locket and embroidered silk purse, Emily's diary of pressed flowers, the strange piece of magic rock and finally a compass tied to a ball of golden yellow silk thread – James recognised them all. The image blurred again but the cloud continued to boil and bubble as Mchawi raised his hands skywards. The mist slowly began to clear but the face that appeared shocked James the most, to Rory and Becky it was a mystery for they had never seen Adam.

"Who is it?" they both asked turning to James. "Do you know?"

"Yes, it's Adam," replied James in disbelief as they all turned toward Mchawi looking for an explanation of the strange vision.

The White Mganga sat on the ground exhausted with the effort and the children had to wait for him to recover his strength. Ziwadi seemed concerned that he was not responding to her chattering, she sat on his head bending down to look into his eyes but they remained vacant as though he was in another place. Her agitation must have aroused Mchawi as he slowly became conscious of the children looking intently at him and with some effort he got to his feet. Becky seemed the most concerned putting her arm around his shoulder and asking if he was alright, James and Rory however, were more interested to learn the meaning of his strange vision.

"Do not concern yourselves my children, Mchawi is fine, it just required such strong magic and I am getting old, it takes me longer to recover."

"But do you know the meaning of everything and *why* Adam's face appeared?" James enquired mystified and anxious to find the answers.

"All in good time James, you will learn everything. First, I must refresh myself and clear my mind with some cool water." They all sat on the ground outside his hut and Mchawi began to explain what had been revealed to him.

"Your friend Adam as yet has no magic powers himself but somehow he was transported back to a time before Emily gained her powers that is why she could not see him – the time was not right."

"But what about all the things that flew out of the trunk?"

"Patience James, I will tell you all that I know. Your friend Adam felt a connection to Emily when he first held the locket containing her hair because she has chosen *him* to right the wrong done to her."

"But why Adam and not James," enquired Becky somewhat crossly, "after all *he* is the one who now has magic powers." James and Rory both nodded in agreement.

"Yes, but Adam has something James does not, his ancestors came from the same village as Emily and the wrong cannot be righted by someone from outside. She has been waiting a long time for all the pieces to come together and now the time would appear to be right. Somewhere in her book of pressed flowers James, you will find a riddle which you must first solve. Within her purse you have already found some old coins," James nodded. "At a time, which will be shown to you, you must take those coins for they will be a payment for Adam. The compass will guide you both to the right time and place, the silk thread will bind you together with Emily."

"What about the magic rock?" James asked.

"At a time in the future Adam will need his own magic power but this is all I know. Maybe when you solve the riddle your questions will be answered."

"Gosh, you learnt all that from the vision," Rory said in amazement.

"Only because there are powers greater than mine who grant me the means to look into the past and the future."

James was now eager to meet up with Adam and find the riddle in Emily's book which he hoped they could solve. After Adam's experience on the rocking horse, he felt sure there would be little difficulty in explaining to him all the things Mchawi had told them. He also wanted to spend some time with his two friends and see what they had done since their adventure on the Sacred Mountain. They said their goodbyes to Mchawi and Ziwadi who jumped up and down with excitement on his shoulder. Soon Mtumwa had transported them back to the waterhole where the horses were patiently waiting beneath the Acacia trees. They sat for a while watching impala and zebra come to drink, James almost wished he could stay there forever when he thought of the cold English winter that lay ahead of him and the possibility, he may find it difficult climbing the Cedar tree if the weather was frosty. Watching the vultures circling high in the sky above he couldn't help breaking the silence to ask what happened when they had lived at Rookery Manor.

"The Cedar tree was always out of bounds when the winter was icy or we had snow," replied Becky. "Our parents never really knew why we loved climbing the Cedar Tree."

"My fault," said Rory with a sheepish grin, "I tried climbing one icy winter, slipped, fell and broke my arm."

"Yes, and Mother went spare, Father forbade us to go anywhere near it in the winter." Becky looked at her brother with mock disapproval.

"I guess if it's a bad winter I won't be able to see much of you both," James said with a note of sadness in his voice.

"But we'll still be here and you will come when winter is over," Becky re-assured him. "You will have lots to tell us about Adam and what you discover about the riddle."

"Yes, that should be exciting," James cheered up, suddenly remembering how eager he had been to go back and tell Adam all that he had learnt from Mchawi.

"Come on James, let's ride across the plains before Mtumwa takes you back to your time." With that Rory climbed onto his horse and soon all three friends were riding through herds of impala and zebra scattering them on all sides. The sun shone down from a blue, cloudless sky and an exhilarating sense of freedom overwhelmed them so they forgot that danger can lurk unseen around every bush on the African plains.

Riding a little way in front Rory was intending to skirt around a small copse of thorn bushes when, without warning his horse reared up into the air and he was thrown to the ground. Stamping its hooves and whinnying loudly it was a miracle Rory avoided being trampled on. Then a loud roaring came from nearby and the horse took off at speed.

"Oh no," exclaimed Becky in horror, "lions – we must have disturbed them." As she and James rode up to where Rory was sat on the ground, winded from his fall.

Sure enough Rory had ridden into the most dangerous situation he could have, a pride of lions feeding on a zebra they had recently killed. Momentarily the lions were as surprised as the children, then a large male began walking menacingly towards them. The pride stopped feeding and turned to face the three friends snarling and showing their fearsome teeth, the message was plain to see. Becky could not hold onto her horse as fear gave it strength and speed so it too sped off across the plains in a cloud of dust leaving the three of them clinging to each other with no-where to run.

"James, do something," Becky pleaded shaking his arm in desperation. "Use your new magic before they kill us too."

James was not at all sure if the magic could work without Mchawi or the magic rock. He thought about calling for the whistle to summon Mtumwa but there wasn't time the lions were only a few feet away. Summoning all his courage James closed his eyes and in imitation if Mchawi raised his hands towards the sky.

"If you really have given me magic power then make the lions afraid of us," he implored, keeping his eyes tightly shut. For a moment nothing happened.

"James, look." Becky was shaking his arm again, surprise in her voice unable to believe what she was seeing.

Opening his eyes James stared in amazement it was as if a wall of fire had sprung up from the ground between them and the lions. Flames flickered and danced yet the ground did not burn nor was there any smoke or smell of burning. The lions appeared confused and afraid pacing up and down as though unsure of what to do. Most of the lionesses turned and fled, stopping to glance behind from time to time. Eventually even the large male's courage left him and he ran after the rest of the pride. Slowly the flames sank into the ground and disappeared. Becky threw her arms around James's neck kissing him on the cheek causing him to blush bright red. Rory smiled a look of relief crossing his face as he tried to get up.

"Are you OK, nothing broken?" asked James attempting to sound as if everything was normal.

"Yes, just a bit bruised, I think. What about you James, *how* did you do that?"

"I don't really know," said James in amazement, "I thought about the whistle to summon Mtumwa for help but there wasn't time so I concentrated hard that if I really did have magic powers then I wanted the lions to be too afraid to attack us and I guess it worked."

"Too right it worked thank goodness." Becky sounded relieved. "Now all you need to do is conjure up our horses so we can go home." As if on cue their horses appeared trotting towards them.

"I definitely didn't do that," said James.

The three friends laughed a little nervously, an overwhelming sense of relief that they were all alive and the danger had passed. Climbing back onto their horses they hurriedly rode across the plains towards the plantation and safety.

As James said goodbye and climbed the Flame Tree he promised to return when he and Adam had solved the riddle Mchawi had spoken of. As he stared into Mtumwa's eyes he couldn't help wondered what would have happened if the magic had not worked. His parents particularly would have no way of knowing what had become of him, he would just have disappeared off the face of the earth. A mental picture of their distress and anguish flashed in front of his eyes and then he was sat in the Cedar Tree, thankfully everything was alright.

Chapter 16 –
The Riddle

It wasn't until the following afternoon that James was able to meet up with Adam who couldn't wait to hear if he had learnt anymore. A whole week had passed since Adam's strange encounter with the Beauregard's and the experience had haunted him every day and even invaded his dreams. In spite of Adam's impatience James made him wait until they were upstairs in his bedroom – he couldn't risk being overheard by his parents. Sitting cross-legged on the floor it was as though Adam had ants in his pants and couldn't keep still.

"'Urry up, James, put me out of me misery, did yeh find out anythin'?"

James lay on his bed and began to tell Adam first about Mchawi, the White Witchdoctor and all the things they learnt from his visions and finally why Emily had not been able to see him. From under his pillow James took out Emily's book which he had taken from the attic earlier.

"Now Mchawi said that there was a riddle hidden somewhere in her book that would guide us as to what to do. Mchawi also told me that it was you Emily had chosen to 'right the wrong' as he called it because your ancestors are from this village and I'm not."

"That's true," said Adam thoughtfully. "Maybe one of 'em were even wiv the people what killed 'er."

"No matter, that's not your fault. Let's look at the book together and see if we can find anything."

Adam climbed up onto the bed and together they began to pour over the pages one at a time but they were nearly at the end before James noticed some words, he was sure hadn't been there before, so small it would have been easy to miss them. The page had a drawing that looked very like the woodland glade with the cave entrance and it was decorated with fern fronds and dry grasses. Written in tiny neat letters were the words:

Glistening bright in the watery deep

Reach within your reward to reap.

"Is that all?" Adam sounded disappointed.

"Maybe there's more on this page." James turned the page over. "Look there's some more writing here."

Ride my brave Prince for the hour is nigh

To pay the huntsman so you can pass by.

"Well, I seen huntsmen in the woods when I was riding Prince but they didn't seem to see me," said Adam.

"Let's see if there's more on the other pages. Yes, look each page has a couple of lines on it. I'll get some paper and a pen; we can write them down and see if it makes any sense." After a few minutes they had written down the whole riddle.

Glistening bright in the watery deep

Reach within your reward to reap.

Ride my brave Prince for the hour is nigh

To pay the huntsman so you can pass by.

Down through the Hollow when frost nips the air

The time must be right for I must be there.

The things that you see will guide you to me

If you heed what they say to set me free.

Set the compass and read it well

To travel through time and cast its spell

Our lives intertwined with a golden thread

`Where the past is the present you carefully tread

The magic is yours so use it with care

Dark forces abound so watch and beware.

As James finished reading Adam let out a loud sigh. "'Ow on earth are we supposed to understand what all that means."

"Well," said James thoughtfully, "some things we already know, so let's start with them. We know who Prince is and you said you had seen huntsmen riding through the woods. It says you have to ride Prince down Frosty Hollow and Mchawi told me that the old coins in the silk purse are to pay the huntsman to let you pass by. He said the golden thread in the trunk was to tie the past and present together."

"OK but what's the reward in the watery deep?" asked Adam somewhat perplexed.

James thought for a while trying to remember what Mchawi had told him. At some point he seemed to think Adam would need his own magic. Turning back to the page where it was written James suddenly exclaimed, "I've got it. Look the drawing is of the cave in the woodland glade and where does that lead too?"

"Yer cellar," replied Adam still mystified.

"Yes, but before that what did we find?"

"That big pool wiv all them shiny rocks." Adam paused as the realisation struck him. "Just like the one in the trunk."

"Exactly," said James feeling rather pleased with himself, "The one that gave Emily her magic powers and Mchawi said you would need your own magic eventually. I think we have to take one from the Glass Lake for you and see what happens."

"OK but it says 'the time must be right' 'cause she's got to be there. 'Ow do we know when Emily's goin' to be there, wherever 'there' is?" Adam still sounded confused.

"Well, the riddle says to 'set the compass and read it well' so there must be something on the compass. Come on let's get it out of the trunk and take a look."

Together the two friends quietly entered the attic and opened Emily's trunk. Adam was reluctant to sit on the rocking horse again in case anything happened, so they both sat on the floor while James took out various items placing them beside him on the floor until he reached the compass. At first glance it appeared like any normal compass with N, S, E and W in large letters but on closer inspection he saw that writing was appearing all around the outer edge and smaller writing in-between. There were two large arrows which could be moved in either direction. Underneath the letter N for north were the words Rookery Manor and next to the E for east the words Frosty Hollow, by the S for south it read Woodland Glade and W for west was The Glass Lake. The inner circle of words read from the top clockwise The Cedar tree, The Messenger, Rookery Woods, The Cave, Village Church, Graveyard, Rookery Manor Cellar and finally The Attic. Beneath the N and Rookery Manor it said 'past' and above S and The Woodland Glade the word 'present'.

"I guess you have to turn the arrows to where you want to go and whether it's in the past or present?" James sounded a little unsure but neither of them could come up with a better explanation.

"Yeah but 'ow will we know when the time's right fer Emily to be there?"

"I don't know." Sighed James looking intently at the compass as though hoping something else would be revealed. "Let's read the riddle again."

Adam picked up the paper they had written the riddle on and read the first few lines.

"I think that means the first thing we must do is get another of the magic rocks for you," suggested James.

"Aye and we 'ave to ride down Frosty 'Ollow when tis frosty," added Adam.

"I remember Mchawi said the time would be revealed to us, so perhaps Emily is going to appear again in the picture," mused James thoughtfully.

"Come on then let's go see," said Adam excitedly because up to now he hadn't seen her picture.

Quietly leaving the attic the boys made their way to the cold bedroom but although they looked longingly at the wall for some time, nothing happened.

"Maybe we need to get a magic rock first," suggested James. Adam's face fell.

"We don't 'ave to go through the dark passage from the cave, do we?"

James thought for a moment. "Well, if we went when Mrs Perkins wasn't here maybe we could climb back through the pantry and into the cellar. If we were quiet and didn't make a mess no one would know, would they."

At that thought Adam's face lit up. "Good idea, let's go."

"I think we'll have to leave it for another time," said James looking out of the window. "It's starting to get dark;

you'll be expected home and Mother will be cooking in the kitchen soon."

Disappointment crossed Adam's face, that would mean another week would go by and he so wanted to solve the mystery but there was little he could do except wait until James returned from school next weekend so they agreed to meet up again the following Saturday afternoon.

Chapter 17 –
A Message from Emily

The week seemed never ending for both boys but particularly Adam who felt school was something to endure anyway rather than to be enjoyed. Soon it would be Christmas and there would be a whole three-week holiday. Adam's family always enjoyed Christmas with plenty of family and friends to enjoy it with. James wasn't sure what his parents had planned for their first Christmas at Rookery Manor. When they had lived in London there had always been plenty of parties, from his parents' friends and business associates to parties for James and his friends.

In the great entrance hall of the school a huge Christmas tree had been erected over the weekend, decorated by the teachers and senior boys. James thought it looked very festive in silvery tones as though it had been sprinkled with frost and snow. His friends Thomas and Patrick appeared at the top of the staircase and hurried down to greet him.

"Hi James," they called out excitely, "doesn't it look great."

"I can't wait for Christmas," said Patrick, "three whole weeks with no school – bliss."

Thomas was eager to know what James would be doing over the holidays.

"Not sure exactly," he replied, "It's the first Christmas since leaving London and my parents haven't said anything yet."

"I guess in a great big manor house like yours there'll be a roaring log fire and lots of present under the tree." Thomas sounded a bit envious but James ignored it thinking the best Christmas present for him and Adam would be to solve the riddle and find out what happens next.

Depositing his fresh clean clothes in the dormitory James and his friends made their way to the first lesson of the day.

Sitting in the dormitory that evening before lights out James wished he could confide in his two friends and tell them about the riddle but he knew they wouldn't understand, even if he told them the whole story from the very beginning. Instead, he allowed himself to be drawn into their excitement about Christmas and how they hoped it would snow. That made James think about the riddle again and how they had to ride down Frosty Hollow 'when frost nips the air'. James smiled to himself picturing Rookery Woods covered in snow, waking up on Christmas morning, sitting in front of a roaring log fire in the sitting room and opening presents with his parents. I wonder if Mrs Perkins will be cooking our Christmas dinner he thought but guessed she would be cooking her own dinner or maybe they celebrated with her sister, Adam's mother and family. He found it hard to settle that night and sleep evaded him long after everyone else had drifted into the land of nod.

The week passed uneventfully and driving home with his father on Friday afternoon he could hardly contain his excitement. Curious to find out if his parents had any plans for Christmas, he talked about what his friends would be doing.

"What will we do this year?" he enquired. Much to his relief his father said they had decided to spend their first Christmas at Rookery Manor quietly, just the three of them and not go anywhere, except perhaps if James wanted, they could go to see the pantomime in Bristol.

"You could even bring Adam with you if you liked," his father suggested.

"Brilliant, that would be fun." James smiled; he wondered if Adam had ever been to see a pantomime. The more his parents liked Adam the better he thought, as it was becoming increasingly obvious that he, Adam and their futures were inextricably linked together with Emily Beauregard.

Opening his bedroom curtains on Saturday morning James looked out to the Cedar Tree and wondered what Rory and Becky would be doing. The sky was grey and overcast, no doubt they would be enjoying blue skies and warm sunshine but he and Adam had an important task to complete later that day so there was no time to day-dream.

Once lunch was cleared away his mother prepared to take a basket of homemade cakes to the village hall for the Christmas Fayre. As his father had offered to help with setting up the tables fortunately for James that left the house empty for him and Adam to visit the Glass Lake. Punctual as always Adam knocked on the kitchen door precisely at 2 o'clock.

"I saw yer Ma and Pa drive away so I knew we'd be alone." Adam threw his coat and scarf over a kitchen chair. "Let's get goin' then, I've waited all week fer today, thought it 'ould never come."

James smiled at Adam's eagerness but he felt excited too and wondered what they would discover. Together they carefully moved the jars and plates from the shelf in front of the concealed door which led to the old wine cellar. Squeezing through they pushed the door which now moved more easily but it still gave a loud creak. Climbing down the steps using the pantry light to guide them, they entered the old cellar. Adam found the light switch revealing the trap door at the far end. Taking hold of the large metal ring they pulled together but at first it didn't seem to move.

"Gosh, were this so 'eavy before?"

"I guess we've just forgotten," replied James straining every muscle when the trap door suddenly sprang open sending them both reeling backwards to fall on the floor in a heap. They looked at each other in surprise before laughing at how funny they must both look. James felt in his pocket and took out the torch he had brought.

"Phew, not broken thank goodness," He breathed a sigh of relief as he switched it on lighting up the blackness below and revealing the stone steps leading down to the cave and Glass Lake.

The steps glistened in the light, it was cold and damp now that winter was here. The boys carefully lowered themselves down finding the steps were now quite slippery. James held tightly to the torch and slowly they made their way down into the cave. It was much darker than the first time they had discovered it as now there were no shafts of sunlight penetrating down from the woodland above. When their eyes became accustomed to the dark the light from the torch reflected off the cave walls now dripping with water and the Glass Lake looked even more forbidding than before.

"Come on James, let's get one of them rocks and get out of 'ere, it gives me the creeps." Adam felt shivers up and down his spine and not just from the cold.

James shone the torch onto the water and reached down until he felt a piece of rock. It glinted and shone even in the darkness of the cave. Adam held his breath and James dropped it into his outstretched hands, as he did so Adam let out a yell of pain and dropped the rock back into the water.

"It burnt me 'and," he exclaimed in disbelief.

"That's what happened to me the first time. When the time is right, you'll find it just sends a warm glow all through your body and then you can do extraordinary magical things." James reached down to retrieve the rock from the water, wrapping it in a piece of cloth and putting it in his pocket.

James shone his torch around the cave one more time before they quickly retraced their steps until they were safely back in the pantry, carefully returning the jars and plates to their original places on the shelf and wiping away their dirty footprints.

"There, no one will ever know a thing," said James feeling satisfied with their efforts. "Come on, let's look at the riddle again."

It was cold in the attic so they took Emily's diary and lay on the floor in James's bedroom.

"Right, we've taken a magic rock so the next thing we 'ave to do is ride Prince but we 'ave to find out when the time's right, 'cause Emily's got to be there." Adam pursed his lips in thought.

James looked puzzled, how were they to find out when the time was right. The riddle didn't tell them only to set the compass well but to where and when?

"I'm going to bring the compass," he said getting up off the floor and leaving Adam looking at the riddle.

Returning with the compass in his hand he felt a strange sensation as he passes the door of the 'cold room'. Pausing a moment, he reached out and turned the door knob, the same mild electric shock ran up his arm as he called out for Adam to come quickly. Wondering what was the matter, Adam scrambled to his feet and hurried out of the bedroom and through the other door where he saw James staring at the wall. He turned to look and there in front of them was a picture, hazy and indistinct at first, then as though a mist had lifted Emily appeared sitting on the rock beside the woodland pool. She turned and smiled, stretching out her hands towards them she slowly opening her fingers to reveal a compass just like the one James had taken from the trunk. As they watched in silence the woodland glade became covered in a layer of icy frost and snowflakes began to fall. Suddenly the compass flew out of Emily's hand and almost filled the picture frame. As they watched the directional arrows began spinning around the face of the compass, faster and faster until James and Adam felt quite dizzy. When it stopped one arrow was pointing straight up to Rookery Manor and the past while the other arrow was moving back and forth between Frosty Hollow and the Woodland Glade, eventually it stopped and pointed to Frosty Hollow. Gradually the picture began to fade and disappeared leaving an empty space on the wall.

Adam was first to speak, "Is someone playin' tricks or did we just see …" his voice trailed off.

"Yes," replied James, "that was a message from Emily."

A little dazed they made their way back to James's bedroom and sat down on the bed. Sitting beside James, Adam let out a loud sigh, "Did yeh understand what it all meant?"

"Maybe, but we won't know if I'm right until we try." James paused for a moment opening his hand to look at the compass.

"Why were it frosty and snowin'?"

"I think she was telling us that the time will be right when the woodland is heavy with frost and it's snowing."

"And when will that be?"

"Your guess is as good as mine Adam. It's winter now so I suppose it could be anytime, we'll just have to wait until it starts snowing then we'll have to ride Prince together."

"What if it 'appens while yer at school?"

"There's only one more week and then we break up for the Christmas holidays so I'll be home until the New Year. We'll just have to hope it happens then."

The boys made plans for Adam to visit Rookery Manor as soon as any snow began to fall and James would prepare the silk purse with the old coins, the ball of golden yellow thread and the compass all ready beside Prince so they wouldn't forget anything. They agreed to wait and see if anything happened and James promised to let Adam know if Emily appeared again or he learnt anything new. It was starting to get dark as Adam walked down the drive and turned towards the village and his home. James closed the front door glad of the warmth inside and wondered what the future had in store for them both, especially Adam. What would he have to do to save Emily from an untimely death and would that mean her spirit could no longer live in Rookery Manor? Suppose the magic stopped and he could no longer visit Rory and Becky, at that thought he felt a cold shiver run down his spine and a deep sadness fell like a blanket over his shoulders.

Chapter 18 –
Snowfall and a Journey Begins

It was the end of term and everyone was looking forward to the Christmas holidays. Friends exchanged presents on the last day after a wonderfully festive school lunch and the whole building seemed to echo with the sound of laughter and Christmas carols. James was thrilled when Patrick and Thomas presented him with a small beautifully wrapped box.

"It's from both of us," said Thomas, "and you're not to open it until Christmas."

A little shyly James handed them each a small gift with the same instructions. Their friendship had helped him settle into a new school and a new life since leaving London. He often wished he could tell them about his adventures in Kenya, Adam and all the magic that surrounded Rookery Manor but he knew they wouldn't understand or believe him and he valued their friendship at school too much.

"Have a great Christmas both of you and I'll see you in January," said James as he waved them goodbye.

"We want to hear all about your holiday too," Patrick shouted after him.

I wonder what that will be thought James as he hurried out to meet his father.

Life had been pretty hectic since the weekend he had seen Adam and there had been no opportunity to see Rory and Becky either. His parents had whisked him off to London to see friends and buy their Christmas presents but now as he lay in bed thinking, he had three whole weeks to do exactly as he liked. The sound of voices downstairs broke into his thoughts and he realised he felt rather hungry. At the thought of Mrs Perkins fried sausages, bacon and eggs James jumped out of bed and quickly threw on his dressing gown. Hurrying down the stairs a cold draught filled the normally warm hallway, the front door was wide open and he could hear his father's voice coming from outside. Wrapping his dressing gown tightly around himself he peered around the door. A post office van was in the driveway and Mr Perkins and his father were carrying a large parcel into the garage. I wonder what that's all about he mused but with the smell of breakfast cooking and the rumble in his tummy James quickly forgot and headed down the hall towards the kitchen.

"There yeh are Master James. Is it breakfast yer after?" Mrs Perkins gave him a knowing smile as she popped some sausages into a pan. "Yer Ma and Pa 'ave already finished theirs. I thought yeh was never comin' down and me and old perks will be off 'ome soon."

"I just didn't feel like getting up this morning."

"Don't blame yeh Master James it's proper parky outside, t'wouldn't surprise me if we 'ad some snow."

The word 'snow' focused James mind on the weekend when he and Adam had seen Emily's picture. Perhaps their adventure would happen before Christmas; the thought gave him goosebumps.

"How can you tell Mrs Perkins?"

"Ooh the look o' the sky mostly," she said while putting breakfast on his plate.

Tucking into his pork sausage made James think of food again. "Will you be cooking *our* Christmas dinner Mrs Perkins?"

Mrs Perkins laughed, "Ooh, no Master James yer Ma'll be doin' that. I'll be cookin' dinner fer Mr Perkins, me and me sisters family – that's Adam's mum and dad yeh know. We takes it in turns each year and tis my turn this Christmas." Her eyes twinkled and she smiled while cleaning the frying pan before putting it away.

Breakfast over James ran upstairs to get dressed. If there was a chance it might snow, he wanted to see Rory and Becky first to tell them all about the riddle they had found just as Mchawi had said and the message that had appeared from Emily. It had been some time now since his last visit to his friends in Kenya and if it should snow who knew how long it would be before he could climb the Cedar tree again.

Knowing his parents were pre-occupied getting ready for Christmas he took advantage and climbed the Cedar tree. Within minutes he was climbing down from the Flame tree into the warmth of Rory and Becky's garden. How nice to feel the sunshine thought James as he watched Mtumwa preening himself on the fence when his two friends came running towards him.

"Great to see you again," said Rory while Becky hugged him as usual.

"We weren't sure when we would see you again after your last visit," she said.

155

"I had to come and tell you that we found the riddle Mchawi told us about and Emily has appeared to Adam and me."

"Ooh do tell us everything," said Becky excitedly.

They sat down on the grass beneath the Flame tree and James began to tell them from the beginning all that he and Adam had discovered. Before he finished Honey, the tame cheetah, came and lay beside him purring like a cat while he gently stroked her head.

"How exciting," exclaimed Becky as James finished telling them everything.

"Gosh, nothing as exciting as that ever happened when we lived at Rookery Manor," said Rory sounding a little disappointed.

"I think it's because of Adam. He seems to be the one chosen by Emily to right the wrong done to her because he comes from the village, which is what Mchawi said. Neither you nor I came from the village we just lived at Rookery Manor but now Adam has become my friend I think that is the connection."

"You could be right," replied Rory and Becky nodded in agreement. "You must let us know what happens."

"I will but I'm not sure how soon I can return and I must go back to my time now before I'm missed. My parents are expecting me to help decorate the Christmas tree."

"I sometimes wish we had a traditional Christmas with snow outside and a roaring log fire just like we used to when we lived at Rookery Manor," Becky said wistfully.

"Mmm but only for Christmas," said James, "the rest of the time I'd rather have your sunshine."

The three friends hugged each other before James climbed back up the Flame tree for Mtumwa to return him to his own time. He turned and waved goodbye as Becky shouted after him, "Come back soon."

James had hardly climbed down from the Cedar tree before he heard his father calling him and knew it was time to decorate the Christmas tree, something he always enjoyed and this year it would be extra special. Over the next few days he eagerly opened the curtains each morning hoping to see snow and although heavy grey clouds drifted across the sky the snowflakes refused to fall just a light dusting of frost which didn't last long. He began to think it was not going to happen before Christmas and only hoped snow did not fall on Christmas Day as he was sure Adam would not be able to visit then.

On the morning of the fifth day after seeing Rory and Becky he climbed slowly out of bed feeling a little dejected, the excitement was wearing off. Opening the curtains to look towards the Cedar Tree he could hardly believe his eyes. The lawn was white and large snowflakes were floating down to cover the branches of the Cedar tree making it look almost magical, like a giant Christmas tree. James stared in amazement with a large smile gradually spreading across his face.

"Magic," he paused looking all around the garden. "If we have guessed right then today is the day our journey to save Emily begins."

He hurried downstairs and into the kitchen. "You were right Mrs Perkins."

"I was. What was I right about Master James?"

"The snow Mrs Perkins, the snow. It's snowing – look." James jumped up and down with excitement as he gazed out of the kitchen window.

"Oh arh," she murmered, "this'll be the first time yeh saw the country white wiv snow I guess." James nodded; he couldn't tell her the real reason for his excitement.

Just then the telephone rang in the hallway and he could hear his mother's voice speaking to someone. A moment later and she came into the kitchen.

"That was your friend Adam. He said he would be coming around this morning to help you build a snowman."

"Oh great," said James, "I'd better get dressed then." And he ran up the stairs two at a time, he knew exactly why Adam was coming.

Chapter 19 – The Meeting

By the time Adam knocked on the kitchen door James had already taken the silk purse filled with old coins, the ball of golden yellow silk thread and the compass out of the trunk and laid them on the floor next to Prince.

"I've got something to show you Adam," said James giving him a conspiratorial wink, "then we can go build an enormous snowman."

"Make sure you dress warmly when you go outside," his mother called after them.

Once in his bedroom James took the magic rocks from their hiding place in his wardrobe and put one in his pocket. Unwrapping the second one from the cloth that had covered it since they took it from the Glass Lake, he held it out to Adam who looked a little unsure.

"Oooh I dunno, it burnt me 'and that first time."

"Yes, but as I said that was because the time wasn't right. It must be the right time now 'cos it's snowing just like Emily told us in the picture. Hold out your hands and we'll hold it together."

Somewhat reluctantly Adam did as James asked and the two boys wrapped their hands around it.

"I can feel it getting' warm," said Adam nervously.

"But it won't burn you. Can you feel the warmth creeping up your arms?" asked James.

"Yeh," replied Adam, "'tis makin' me feel warm all over."

The rock glowed brightly between their hands for some moments before it turned cold just as it had when James and Mchawi had held it all those weeks before.

"Put it in your pocket and keep it safe, it will never harm you again. Now let's go ride Prince and make some magic to save Emily."

Creeping along the landing they quietly opened the door to the attic and climbed the stairs. It was bitterly cold and they were both glad they had decided to wear their coats and scarves. James picked up the items from the floor putting the silk purse in his pocket and handing the ball of golden yellow silk thread to Adam.

"Now before we ride Prince I must set the compass." James thought for a minute as he moved the arrows. "One arrow must point to Rookery Manor in the past." Adam nodded in agreement as James set the arrow in place.

"And the other one went there," said Adam impatiently pointing to Frosty Hollow.

James positioned the second arrow making sure it pointed to Frosty Hollow in the past. Holding tightly to the compass he climbed up onto the rocking horse while Adam climbed up behind him.

"Are we ready?" asked James taking a deep breath as Adam nodded. Clutching the compass, he took hold of Princes reins and the boys began to rock back and forth.

"Giddy-up Prince take us to Emily." James began to rock faster and faster. He could feel Adam's arms tightening around his waist as the wind began to rush past their faces and the attic disappeared. Suspended for a moment in nothingness and then they were galloping through the woods white with snow and Prince had become a magnificent white stallion, living and breathing his muscles rippling beneath them.

"It's just like it 'appened before," Adam shouted in James's ear as they sped on deeper and deeper into the woods.

The icy wind whistled past their ears and stung their eyes, crouching low over Prince's flowing mane they didn't realise they were almost at Frosty Hollow until he came to a sudden stop. They sat up peering from behind Prince's head. In front of them sat a rider on a jet-black horse, his riding boots just visible beneath a thick fur cloak, ornate leather gloves almost up to his elbows held onto the horse's reins.

"Halt," a voice boomed out at them. "No one can pass the Huntsman until they pay the levy." His face in shadow beneath a large brimmed hat, only his eyes seemed to glare at them like two balls of fiery light.

James could feel Adam's grip tightening as he took the silk purse out of his pocket.

"How much is the levy?" James could hear his voice trembling.

"How much have you got?" the voice boomed out again and the eyes seemed to glow even more brightly.

James opened the purse and took out the coins that were inside. Opening his hand to show the Huntsman who nodded in approval and quickly scooped them all up.

"Pass, be on your way but take care to cross my path again lest your life be forfeit."

James urged Prince onward, his heart thumping, not sure what the Huntsman had meant, it had sounded threatening but that was something Emily had not warned them about.

"I didn't like the sound of 'im," whispered Adam, "and if we can't cross his path again 'ow are we goin' to get back?"

"Let's worry about that later, so far everything is as we were told by Emily."

Prince moved more slowly down Frosty Hollow as here the snow lay deeper and the branches glistened white with frost. Entering the Woodland Glade, it looked almost like a fairy grotto and at first appeared silent and empty. Neither James nor Adam had ever seen it like this, there had always been the sound of birds and the rustle of a gentle breeze through the leaves but now everything was still, no sound, no movement except Prince as he slowly walked towards the centre. He pawed the ground and snorted, shaking his mane as though to clear it of snow and then, there she was, Emily sitting beside the now frozen pool wrapped in a white fur cloak and hood. She seemed to be part of the woodland, invisible until she moved and spoke. Reaching out a delicate gloved hand she stroked Prince lovingly on his muzzle.

"My Prince, you have brought them to me as I knew you would." Emily turned to James and Adam her smile warm and welcome as she invited them to come down.

"She can see me, she can see me," Adam repeated, his eyes full of wonder.

"Yes Adam, I can see you both because you followed the instructions I gave you and came at the proper time." Her voice soft and tender bewitching them both. "Come, let's go inside the cave where it is much warmer and we have so much to talk about."

They followed her into the cave and gasped in amazement at what they saw.

"It never looked like this when we came 'ere before." Adam's eyes seemed to pop out of his head as they stared around. The cave appeared much bigger than before and it was filled with candles glowing brightly from the many ledges around the cave walls. In the centre glowed a warm log fire, yet there was no smoke, the flames flickered and danced yet the wood didn't burn. Must be magic thought Adam.

Emily laughed at their obvious confusion. "Of course, it didn't look like this, then it was natural, now it is as *I* wish it."

They sat down glad of the warmth to ease the aching cold from the woods.

"I don't understand all the things that have happened – the magic rocks, how we can travel back in time and why we are here? Why me and Adam?"

"All in good time you will understand everything," Emily assured them. She began to tell them about her life how happy and wonderful it had been for many years. They learnt Emily had been born at Rookery Manor but never knew her mother as she had died a few days later. When she was seven her father had brought Prince home for her birthday, it had been the most wonderful present ever. As her confidence grew, she and Prince would ride through the woods most days coming to the woodland glade to watch the animals and listen to the birds. Eventually they lost their fear of her and became her companions.

"But 'ow did yeh know to speak wiv 'em?" asked Adam.

"Like you both, I discovered the magic rocks in the Glass Lake and they gave me certain powers which you already know."

"Yeah but … but 'ow did yeh know the Glass Lake were there?"

Emily smiled at Adam's confusion and laid her hand gently on his, making him blush like a ripe tomato.

"I will explain from the beginning so you will understand everything for it is important that you do."

Long before she was born her father, Edgar Charles Beauregard had become a successful and wealthy merchant bringing silks and expensive perfumes from the Far East. Bristol had become a thriving port and he wanted to live within easy reach but in the country. He found a small cottage on a large piece of land almost surrounded by woodland and close to a busy village. Although the cottage was too small for his needs the situation was perfect and he decided to build Rookery Manor where the cottage had stood as a fitting home for his new wife, Emily's mother, Constance Francine Beauregard. Both her parents were part French which accounted for their names.

Edgar Beauregard however, at the time had not realised that the previous occupants of Rookery Cottage were smugglers and had a secret passage leading from the cellar to the centre of the woods. When her father destroyed the cottage to build his manor house, he created enemies among those men in the village who had made money from smuggling anything from the deer and wild boar in the woods to even people. The cottage and the woodland had made the ideal place from which to run their smuggling activities but now her father had made it impossible. Emily of course knew nothing of this until many years later when she discovered the Glass Lake and the magical stones that shone beneath its surface.

"But how did the smugglers not find the magic stones like you did?" asked James.

Emily explained that the Guardians of the Lake only permit the chosen ones to see them. It was only after she died and took on her spirit form that the Guardians revealed themselves to her and the powers she possessed became greater.

"So, who or what are the Guardians of the Lake, 'cause we ain't never seen nothin'?" asked Adam.

"You would not have seen anything because you were both chosen ones and were no threat. The Guardians take on the form of bats who live in the cave and emerge only at night to feed in the woods. People are afraid of bats and associate them with witchcraft so this keeps the lake safe. The smugglers only used the passage for their illegal activities so there was little danger they would find the magic rocks in the lake."

"I ain't never goin' there again," exclaimed Adam shivering. "I don't like bats."

Emily laughed and assured them both they had nothing to fear from the Guardians of the Glass Lake. James was puzzled as to how Emily could speak to them now but in Rookery Manor she always appeared in the picture and never spoke and why did that room always feel so cold?

"That was my room James and where I died," her voice faltered slightly, "that's why it always feels cold to you. Within the house I am not able to speak but here in the woods my voice returns to me so I can talk to the animals and now to you both," she paused for a moment and a look of sadness crept into her eyes. "You see I can never leave Rookery Manor it is only because of the passage from the Glass Lake to this woodland glade I can escape to visit the woods at all. It has been this way for so long and I want so much to be free. There are times when I wish …" Her voice trailed away and the sadness in her eyes enveloped them all.

Both James and Adam knew she was thinking about the visions of future events and the ultimate consequences for her and her father.

"Yeh were not to know village folk would hate yeh for it. It were meant to warn 'em about things what were goin' to 'appen. They 'ad no right to … do what they did ter yer." Adam had been about to say 'kill you' but realised it wouldn't sound right since they were talking face to face.

Taking Adam's hand, Emily smiled softly at him. "My dear, dear friend how long I have waited for you to come to my rescue." At which point Adam blushed even more than before.

James felt almost like an intruder and not sure what to do, he coughed loudly.

"James without you none of this would be possible. If you had not come to live at Rookery Manor the link between the three of us would not exist and who knows how much longer I would have had to wait for all things to come together," she paused as if to collect her thoughts. "Now we must waste no more time for I need to tell you what you must do and when."

She asked James if he had brought the ball of golden yellow silk thread, he nodded and Adam took it from his pocket handing it to Emily not sure what she intended to do. Nestled in the palm of her hand she withdrew a length of golden thread tying it first to Adam's wrist then another length to James's wrist and finally she wrapped a piece around her own.

"Now we are bound together in friendship for all eternity – a bond which no mortal man can break."

Her words reminded James that Mchawi had said this was the purpose of the ball of silk thread. It was Adam who voiced the thought in both their minds.

"What exactly do we 'ave ter do to save yer life. Will it be dangerous?"

"For now, you must ride Prince back to the future but at the first stroke of midnight before the start of New Year's Day you must return to the woods for this is the magic hour when all things become possible. It is only then you can avenge my death and that of my father," she sighed deeply and her lips trembled with emotion before she continued. "You must remember these things before you ride my Prince to the woods again. Tie the silk thread around your wrists, set the compass and bring with you the magic stones, the purse to pay the Huntsman and this time also bring the box of dragonflies."

James then remembered they had no more coins; the Huntsman had taken them all.

"Give me the purse," she asked gently. "You will not need them now to go back but I will fill the purse for your return." With that she placed her hand into the purse and the clink of many coins could be heard. "Hurry, for I must leave you now. Do not forget anything and beware the dark forces. Do not be late …" Her voice drifted away and she disappeared.

James and Adam looked at each puzzled, they knew what they had to bring and when but what they had to do was still a mystery.

"I guess Emily will tell us." But James sounded unsure.

They left the cave and Prince was waiting patiently to take them back to Rookery Manor. In no time at all they were back in the attic as though it had never happened.

Sounding a little concerned and anxious Adam said, "'Ow are we both goin' ter be in yer attic at midnight on New Year's Day?"

"I'm not sure yet," replied James, "but I'll think of something – we have to."

Chapter 20 –
Dragonflies and Dragons

Waking up on Christmas morning James hurried downstairs to find piles of beautifully wrapped parcels under the Christmas tree in the lounge. His father was lighting a log fire in the Inglenook fireplace and it looked so warm and cosy in spite of the snow outside.

"There, we're going to have a real traditional country Christmas this year," said his father beaming broadly, "just the three of us, eh James."

Once breakfast was finished, they returned to the lounge and began to open presents sitting in front of the roaring log fire. There were so many parcels to unwrap it wasn't long before the carpet was covered in pretty Christmas paper and ribbons. Sitting between his mother and father on the large settee James couldn't remember a better Christmas nor one where he had felt happier.

"Now James, there's just one more special present for you in the garage," said his father, "let's go and see what it is, shall we?"

Opening the garage door, at first James could only see his father's car, then when the light was switched on, he saw at the end a gleaming new bicycle.

"We thought you might like to have a bicycle to ride around the village and to visit Adam's house. Do you like it?" His mother had now come out of the house and joined them both in the garage.

"It's great," said James, hugging both his parents in turn. "I can ride to visit Adam when Christmas is over, it will be so much quicker than walking."

On returning to the house the thought of Adam brought back the nagging question of how he and Adam were to get together on New Year's Eve and be in the attic at precisely midnight. Oh well there was a whole week to think about it so for now he would just enjoy the moment.

The answer to James's problem came from his mother a couple of days later when she announced that they were going to have friends down from London to celebrate New Year with a party.

"Some of them will be staying overnight and we thought you might like to invite Adam for a sleep-over so you won't feel left out."

"Brilliant," said James hugging his mother in his excitement. I couldn't have worked it out better myself he thought and rushed off to tell Adam on the telephone leaving his mother a little bemused.

The boys could hardly contain their excitement and each day seemed to last forever. James found it hard to sleep and Adam continued to worry about what they were actually supposed to do. Two days before New Year's Eve James felt particularly restless, his parents were pre-occupied in arranging their party and the arrival of friends from London. His mother was busy making sure everything was ready and in order, after all this would be the first time they would see

Rookery Manor and she wanted them to be suitably impressed.

James and Adam had met up after Christmas but they still had no clue as to what they have to do apart from the instructions Emily had already given them before she had disappeared. Adam had wondered what the box of dragonflies were for – what good would they be in fighting the dark forces she had spoken about, whatever those forces were?

To quell the butterflies in his stomach James decided to prepare all the items they would need and place them on the attic floor beside Prince. Returning to his bedroom he couldn't resist the temptation to look into the 'cold room' which was now ready for his parent's guests. He looked hopefully at the wall where Emily's picture had usually appeared but it remained blank. He couldn't help voicing aloud his thoughts, "I wish you would tell me what we actually have to do tomorrow night when we ride Prince to the woods."

As if in answer to his wish a picture began to form but all he could see were dark brooding grey clouds that appeared to boil as though a thunderstorm was threatening. He stared at the wall transfixed when out of the clouds flew a piece of white paper which fluttered to the floor beside his feet. James bent down to pick it up and carefully unwrapped the folded paper to reveal some writing. Feeling sure it must have come from Emily he hurried to his room and lying on the bed began to read the final instructions from Emily that they had been hoping for.

Reminding them to set the compass as before and bring the purse to pay the Huntsman, she then wrote, "You must both place your magic rock into a pocket for you may need it to give extra powers to your task. Before you ride Prince tie the golden yellow silk thread around your wrists and do *not* forget the box of dragonflies as without their help you may be defeated by the dark forces. You must be ready to ride Prince precisely at the first stroke of midnight, not a moment before and not a moment after. James you must remember these magic words that will bring the dragonflies to life when you release them into the air – you will know when the moment is right.

Dragonfly, dragonfly, fly higher and higher

Out of your jaws stream a deadly fire

Wings glisten bright in your fiery light

As vengeance you seek for Emily's plight.

You and Adam now have the powers to defeat my enemies, use them well for whatever you wish to happen, it will be so. The Woodland Glade is your destination."

James read and re-read the words on the paper until it was as if they were burnt into his brain. He must ring Adam and tell him what had happened.

New Year's Eve dawned bright and sunny although the snow remained blanketing the countryside and everything around. Adam arrived in the afternoon and the two boys spent the next few hours in James's bedroom talking about all the things that had happened recently and wondering what would be the outcome of the night's adventure. His parent's friends began arriving and soon the party was well underway. James and Adam dutifully mingled for a while and ate far too much food but it was a party after all his mother said and they could stay up late if they wanted. After what seemed an appropriate length of time the boy's said 'goodnight' and wishing everyone a Happy New Year hurried upstairs to James's bedroom.

They set about putting pillows and cushions under the duvets to make it look in the dark as if they were tucked up and fast asleep in bed should either of his parents check up on them. Taking a piece of golden yellow silk thread each, they tied it around their wrists just as Emily had instructed them. James took the magic rock from its hiding place on a shelf and placed it in his pocket.

"You've brought yours haven't you Adam?" James said anxiously wondering if he should have reminded him early in case he forgot.

"Course I 'ave, wouldn't forget that now would I." His voice sounding a little indignant as he removed it from his pocket, the strange metal glinting in the bedroom light.

"Good," said James thankfully, "everything else is ready in the attic, we just have to set the compass" – he looked at the bedside clock – "11.30, I think we should put on our warm coats and scarves because it will probably be cold." James opened his bedroom door to listen. "They'll never hear us with all that noise downstairs but we'll know when it's midnight 'cause the church bells will ring." Adam nodded in agreement.

They crept quietly along the landing, opened the door to the attic and slipped inside. James had brought a torch to lighten up the gloom and shone it onto Prince and the items he had carefully laid on the floor previously. Picking up the compass he set it once more to Frosty Hollow in the past and placed it in his pocket with the silk purse containing the money to pay the Huntsman. He felt in his other pocket to make sure the magic rock was still there.

"Here Adam you'd better hold the box of dragonflies. Come on let's get on Prince so we are ready once midnight begins to strike." James got up first and sat holding the reins while Adam climbed up behind holding onto James with one hand and clutching the box of dragonflies with the other.

"Gosh, I feel like there's a thousand butterflies in me stomach," he said not quite believing what was happening.

"Me too," replied James a little nervously as they heard a loud cheering from downstairs and the church bells began to chime.

"Are you ready?"

"Yeh," replied Adam hoarsely as the church bells rang out heralding a new year.

"Hold tight. Giddy-up Prince take us to Frosty Hollow."

A cold wind swept passed their heads as Prince seemed to gather speed and suddenly, as before, they were riding through the woods only this time there was no snow instead the first signs of autumn were beginning to show. Onward Prince sped until out of no-where the Huntsman appeared before them causing Prince to rear up and Adam to drop the box of dragonflies.

"Halt," said the shadowy figure, "no one can pass the Huntsman until they pay the levy."

Adam was desperately whispering in James's ear. "The box of dragonflies, it flew out me 'and when Prince reared up – what'll we do?"

The Huntsman was holding out a gloved hand and his eyes flashed like fire beneath the broad brim of his hat. James was trying to get the silk purse out of his pocket as he turned to Adam.

"Can you see it?"

"Yeh, not sure if the lid's still on though."

"Try your magic. Hold out your hands and call dragonflies come. See what happens but be confident it'll work."

The Huntsman pointed angrily at his outstretched hand. "The levy or you will not pass."

James nervously handed him the coins beginning to worry that it was all going wrong. He heard Adam make his first attempt at magic hoping his voice sounded more confident than he felt. "Dragonflies come," he commanded as he held out his hands – nothing happened. The Huntsman began to laugh and his eyes seemed to glow brighter as he moved to pick up the box of dragonflies.

"Oh no," groaned Adam slipping off Prince's back and attempting to take the box from the Huntsman.

"What'll you give me for this box?" he sneered holding it in the air too high for Adam to reach.

Prince snorted, shook his head and reared up to knock the Huntsman to the ground causing the box to fly in the air once again. James wrapped his arms around Princes' neck and hung on tightly watching in dismay as the lid flew off and the dragonflies fell to the ground. Adam rushed to pick them up, returning them to the box before handing it too James while he climbed up onto Prince's back again.

"I think I got 'em all and they're OK."

"Good boy Prince," said James relieved patting the horse's neck.

The Huntsman lay on the ground clutching his stomach and glaring at them all, too winded to do anything except to mouth what seemed like some evil curse. The boys didn't stay to find out as Prince galloped on down Frosty Hollow at speed slowing down just before they came to the Woodland Glade and stood within the shadow of the trees, hidden from view.

They could hear muffled voices but until they got down and peered from behind the trunk of a large Oak tree, they could not see who was there. Instinctively James put a finger to his lips in case Adam should blurt out the word 'smugglers'.

In the clearing not far from the cave entrance a log fire was burning, its smoke curling lazily upwards through the trees. Around the fire sat ten men dressed in old dark shabby clothes, scarves around their necks and hats hiding their faces, deep in conversation.

James turned to Adam and whispered in his ear, "We need to find a way to get near enough to hear what they are saying," Adam nodded and pointed to some bushes quite close to the cave.

If they remained hidden within the woodland surrounding the glade and crouched low it would just be possible to reach the bushes without being seen. James took the magic rock from his pocket and signalled for Adam to do the same – they needed to be sure their magic was strong. Holding it in their hands and feeling the warm glow creeping all over their body, Adam nodded as it turned cold and they both placed the rocks back into their pockets.

James turned to Prince who was standing quietly nearby and stroking his muzzle whispered, "Stay here in the shadows Princes and wait for us."

Crouching low to the ground they crept from one tree to another until they had almost reached the bushes beside the cave when James narrowly missed standing on some dry twigs which would have alerted the smugglers to their presence.

"Phew, that was close," he whispered.

Adam picked up two of the largest sticks handing one to James indicating they could use them to hit with if necessary. They were now close enough to hear what was being said. It was also clear that the men carried pistols and one was waving a large knife in the air, its blade shining in the light from the flames. The man seemed to be the leader, he had a swarthy appearance and a dark beard which covered half his face.

"Them Beauregards 'as got ter go. They been interferin' in our business fer far too long," his voice rose in anger.

"Yeh, yeh," the other men agreed. "But 'ow we goin ter do it?" asked one, "we can't shoot 'em or folks 'ould know it were us."

"We could poison 'em," replied another with an evil sneer on his face. "There be plenty o' mushrooms in this 'er wood. We could mix good 'uns wiv bad 'uns, they'd never know."

"But 'ow do we get 'em to eat 'em?" asked the leader.

"I knows their 'ousekeeper," the man replied, "she be sweet on me an' I can give 'er a basket o' mushrooms, she won't never know," he sounded pleased with himself and a smirk crossed his face.

This was far too much for Adam who ran out into the clearing waving his stick and shouting. James had to do something quick and pointed to the fire causing it to explode like a hundred fireworks sending sparks high into the air. To Adam's amazement his anger had empowered him and out from the end of his stick came shiny silver arrows that stung the smugglers like a cloud of biting insects.

Taking their pistols some of the men began firing at Adam but their bullets just exploded in the air like the sparks from the fire. James knew it was time to release the dragonflies, he opened the lid of the box and spoke the magic words.

"Dragonfly, dragonfly, fly higher and higher
Out of your jaws streams a deadly fire.
Wings glisten bright in your fiery light
As vengeance you seek for Emily's plight."

The dragonflies stirred and their wings began to beat faster and faster as they rose into the air climbing high above the woodland glade. There was a flash of brilliant light and the sound like a clap of thunder stopping the smugglers in their tracks. Everyone looked up as out from the light came a horde of orange red dragons breathing a deadly fire from their open jaws.

James and Adam felt the powerful magic fill them with confidence and they began shouting, "This is vengeance for killing Emily Beauregard."

The dragons swooped down among the smugglers who seemed rooted to the spot unable to believe what they were seeing. Some started firing their pistols but as before the bullets just exploded into the air and the area of woodland gradually became scorched from the fire breathing dragons.

The leader of the smugglers ran towards the cave entrance calling his men to follow while the dragons continued to rain deadly fire down on them. Some escaped the flames running into the cave so Adam and James gave chase, they had no intention of letting anyone escape. They could hear men's voices ahead in the passageway which was now lit by torches held in metal brackets on the cave walls. Adam was still waving his stick and shouting, the little silver arrows flying down the passage in front of him.

Ahead they heard screams and terrible sounds coming from the Glass Lake – what could be happening? As soon as the boys burst into the large cave it was clear, the remaining smugglers were being attacked by ferocious bats, the Guardians of the Glass Lake. The men were trapped, there was nowhere to escape. Emily's father had long since locked the trap door into the cellar of Rookery Manor to prevent it being used again. The men were being stabbed by Adam's arrows, bitten mercilessly by the bats and in an attempt to escape the continuous onslaught they jumped into the cold, dark icy waters of the lake. Unable to swim they thrashed about wildly but all gradually sank below the surface and disappeared, the water returned to a still and silent mirror of glass. No one knew how deep the lake was nor if any horrible creatures lurked within its depths – they would never be seen again. At last Emily's murder and her father's death had been avenged.

Emerging into the light of the woodland glade James and Adam sat down with a sense of relief, hardly able to believe what had just happened. Prince was drinking at the little pool and every trace of the smugglers; their fire and the dragons had vanished.

"Did that just 'appen or was we dreamin'?"

"Yes," replied James his voice a mixture of disbelief and excitement. "We really did that Adam, you and me together."

"But them dragonflies, I never imagined them turnin' into real fire breathin' dragons." Adam was shaking his head in amazement still not quite believing what had happened.

"Now we know why Emily insisted that we bring them. I wonder what has happened to them?" James looked around as though expecting to see them somewhere in the Woodland Glade. "You were brilliant Adam; how did you get those arrows to come out of your stick?"

"Not sure," replied Adam a little mystified. "I just wanted to stop them smugglers and hurt them. Next thing I know them arrows is firin' out the end o' me stick."

The boys began to laugh at the memory with a sense of relief at the outcome and their laughter echoing around the glade like a chorus of silver bells chiming the start of a celebration. They had not noticed that Prince was standing beside them and Emily was holding his reins, stroking his muzzle and talking softly in his ear. It was Adam who became aware of her presence first and stopped laughing, his mouth open in surprise as he nudged James on the arm who looked up, clutching his stomach which ached from their laughter.

"My brave, brave hero's I can never thank you enough for coming to my rescue. My spirit can now rest in peace and I can fulfil my destiny as you will both do yours." Emily smiled and hugged them both in turn, Adam blushing like a ripe tomato. She turned to James and from behind her back produced a box they both recognised. "Here you are James, the dragonflies are now back in their box to await another time when they may be needed."

Emily sat down beside them for a moment to re-assure them her presence would always remain at Rookery Manor and the magic would never leave them.

"You must use this power you now possess wisely, never abuse it or the power will leave you forever." She reached forward and touched the golden silk thread around their wrists. "Remember this thread ties our friendship together and no mortal man can break it. Treasure these moments and never forget for they will guide your destiny as they do mine. Now you must ride my Prince back to your time for I must leave you." She rose to her feet and with one last radiant smile, disappeared.

"What now?" Adam sounded as deflated as he felt, as though someone had burst his balloon.

"Do as she said, ride Prince back to our time and eventually the future will reveal itself." He paused a little unsure of his own words. "We saved Emily and destroyed her enemies; we still have our magic powers and we've both gained a true friend."

"Yeah," said Adam smiling once again. "That's the best Christmas present ever." To which James heartily agreed.

A great feeling of satisfaction welled up inside him and the broadest smile creased his face as he looked down at the golden silk thread tied around his wrist – he, Adam and Emily would forever be tied together in an unbreakable bond of friendship. He could hardly wait for the New Year when he would tell Rory and Becky all about their adventure.

Ruth Baker Walton